| CASUALTY |

Casualty |

Zechariah J. Cline

ISBN #: 9798375243122

| author's note

This is an original story I wrote shortly after the first Diamond Kane mystery novel.

Hopefully it is as good.

Enjoy.

Dedicated to the men and women of law enforcement.

Thank you for what you do every day.

Even the dirty cops.

Prologue |

The shadows cast in by the moonlight filtered through the curtains, cascading along the bed, filling the room in a dim brightness. The oak floor was shining in a hue and the body on the bed lay awkwardly posed, left arm draped, fingertip dripping crimson onto the beige carpeting.

The man stood at the foot of the bed, watching the corpse grow old and decay. He held his gun, his weapon of choice poised and ready to shoot again, although there was no point in that now. The person was dead. The next step would take place and then there would be a reason for murder.

As he watched the blood pool on the carpet, he felt his reason for being here understood and being satisfied with the matter in which it had taken place, he left the room and the house behind.

Hours ticked by. The home lay empty and vacant, save for the body as it began to smell. The sound of the cars passing by outside were the only noise to fill the void and the empty words to have been spoken were left unuttered by no one. The killer had left his mark.

For whatever purpose had been said, there was a reason for his killing. The victim was innocent, yes, the woman a young pawn in his game. If she had been elsewhere this would have not worked. The truth behind her reason for existing in his life, as someone he knew, as someone he had known, no longer mattered.

Her body lay on the bed, shattered, broken, a piece of nothingness and a soul that had been taken. The bullet had entered her chest and in doing so, ended her life. The change in the pattern of her ways, the path she had taken had led her here. She would not be able to leave.

As the dawn approached and the light again filtered cleanly through the blinds, the sight of the body was in full view for anyone to see. The sound of footfalls in the hallway echoed as the next person to enter the home came to the room to find the woman dead.

Her scream filled the house. It was her scream that alerted the neighbors the call the police.

A victim had been killed.

A victim had been found.

I |

Detective Diamond Kane stood in the doorway, watching the technicians work on the body. The sign beheld was something she could handle, although the smell of blood was heavy in the air. Next to her, her partner, also her lover, Detective Jayson Bryant looked grim. His eyes stared over the stained carpet.

"It's never gonna come out of the floor," he said. "They'll have to tear it up and redo it all."

"I hope that's not your concern," she said.

Bryant met her eyes. "Of course, it's not."

Diamond looked back at the body and watched the nearest man take a picture as the people surrounding it stepped back. The body was illuminated in a bright flash before the dim. She watched one of the techs use a tool to dig under the fingernails for evidence. Staring back at the face she wondered what the woman had been thinking as she died? Had there been any consolation as to hope in that there would be justice?

She prayed there always was.

As the team finished up, Diamond stepped back to let them through the door and then walking into the room, watched where the markers told her to step, seeing the pool of red having dried and the coagulation of crimson on the woman's arm, running down to her finger.

"Do we have a name?" Bryant asked.

Diamond shook her head. "No," she said. Crouching down to look at the features which remained vacant, blank staring, she eyed the jawline and teeth. Seeing the mouth and the lips she noticed something inside the tongue. Pulling on a pair of gloves she gently opened the victim's mouth and lifting the tongue found something resting beneath it. Damp and stained, the tiny piece of paper held a message printed in black ink.

"What is that?" Bryant said.

"A note," Diamond said.

"To who?"

Carefully, Diamond peeled open the flap and seeing the saliva having dried threatening to ruin the print, she slowly continued and finally holding it open, held it to the light. Her eyes squinted as she read:

The cat and mouse came out to play. The mouse grew stronger every day.

The cat grew weak, the mouse had fun. Until the cat was done and done.

The mouse enjoyed the rivalry. The simple things that you and me.

Have always had between ourselves. The game's begun so let's pray tell.

"What does it say?" Bryant looked at the note and Diamond shook her head. He saw the look on her face.

"The murderer is taunting us," she said. "He wants us to play his game." Standing up she found an evidence bag and placing the note inside, looked at the body. The final words of the message played in her head.

The game's begun so let's pray tell.

She looked at Bryant nodded.

Let the investigation begin.

II |

Lieutenant Dawson Sheppard sat at his desk, sorting through the files that still existed on the last cases. He wondered, as he grew closer to retirement, what he was going to do with the rest of his life. Whether it would be death to take him early, or that he would grow bored and return to work. He didn't care to leave this all behind just yet.

Hearing the news about the murder in the house in East Side, he had grown concerned. Getting the call from Detective Kane about the note found in the victim's mouth, he wondered what the ploy was, and what the killer was up to. The sooner they found out who the victim was, they could find out connections. The body was being moved to the morgue this afternoon after the crime scene was officially cleared and then it would be time to have Detective Kane and Detective Bryant work more on the outside line of this case.

Whatever it was, the matter of which the murderer had staged this crime was enough to chill him. It was almost familiar.

Sheppard sipped his coffee and sat back in his chair, holding his mug. As he looked at the door he rested his fingers on the armrest, closing his eyes and thinking back to the time when he was a cop in uniform, just a boy in blue working a scene where a family had been shot dead. Their child, a young boy with dark blonde hair and teary brown eyes was standing in the middle of the room crying.

Sheppard sipped more coffee, remembering the sound. It had been pained, it had been filled with agony. As he recalled the boy's look of hope that everything would be all right, he thought of the fact that the killer who had shot the parents had left one note each, in the parent's mouths.

He could remember each held words that deflected each other.

The father's was: *Life.*

The mother's was: *Death.*

Chillingly so, the matter was out of his hands and he could do nothing about. The next evening, the killer was found and later tried. He plead not guilty. The boy was in the court room when the jury read the verdict.

Not guilty.

The man walked free. A criminal, a person that Sheppard knew had done wrong. The next evening, he had gone to the boy's new adopted home and seen him. He was not the same. He seemed upset, and troubled by the matter.

"I'm sorry, son," he said. "I did everything I could."

The kid hugged his new mother, hiding behind her. The woman sighed, touching his head, gently smoothing his hair.

"Thank you, officer," she said. "That'll be all, then."

Sheppard left the house behind, considering the fact that he had nothing he could do to fix this. Any way he could have reprimanded the situation enough to be right.

Driving along the road he had followed to get to the boy's house, he remembered the address in his mind from the case file on his desk. Driving East, he headed through traffic and downtown, traveling past the business on Superior Street before turning up 21st and turning onto 5th Street, he parked in front of the two-story stucco. There was no light on, and the windows were dark. As he stepped out of his cruiser, gun drawn, he walked up the sidewalk to the door and reaching the step, stared at the handle. Knowing it to be locked, he pulled on a pair of gloves and then taking hold of the knob, turned it, and pushing with all his force, heard the frame split and crack.

One more push, he thought.

Heaving all his weight, he forced the door in and with a splintering noise, it opened. Stepping into the entryway, he walked through to the stairs, pulling out his gun as he looked into the living room, seeing no one on the couch. Breathing quietly, he ascended each step carefully, moving with careful grace. As he reached the landing, he pointed the barrel and his sights up towards the hallway and seeing no one, continued up the stairs.

The hall was dark, the shadows dancing like supernatural beings that seemed to taunt him as he walked along the carpet. Seeing the door at the end of the hallway cracked and the sliver of moonlight inside filtering to cast a beam over the floor. Sheppard moved towards the sliver of light and keeping his eyes on the gap where he could see the form of someone sleeping in bed, he gently nudged the door open. It creaked on unoiled hinges, the sound loud in his ears.

The bed occupant stirred, groaning before turning onto their back.

Silence.

Sheppard breathed a sigh of relief. As he stepped across the threshold, he looked at the man's face, seeing the familiar features. A criminal in slumber, his rest undisturbed, for the moment anyway, and as he crossed to the bed, he stared at him. Coldly he felt the chill inside his heart, a welcoming demand to make his move. As he stared at the face, peaceful as it shouldn't be, he felt rage. The man was a criminal. He had gotten away and with evidence against him.

Reaching over the body, Sheppard took the pillow that was there, then, as he placed it over the man's face, he pressed the barrel of the gun into the spot where the head was.

He pulled the trigger.

Seated at his desk, Sheppard bit his tongue as he thought about his past a little longer. Then, focusing on the case that was now, he prayed his memory did not fail him.

For the sake of having sinned in the past, he hoped he would not pay for it.

The phone on his desk rang as he picked up and answered. The body was ready to be transported to the morgue. He replied that he understood and hung up. Staring at his empty mug he wondered if his two detectives could handle this. Maybe they weren't ready. The possibility of the fact that he didn't trust them was a reality. He wanted to allow them to have freedom when they worked a case. If it mattered that much to the cause, he was willing to let it slide.

In the end, his concern was towards the truth. If his past was coming back to haunt him, he couldn't tell anyone.

Not yet.

III |

Iris Kane sat on her bed, strumming her guitar, and listening to the tune of music playing from the speakers on her phone set on her desk. The small, but powerful sound filled her room as she listened to Howie Day sing "She Says." The tune was emotional and it filled her ears with the beat of a heart she felt was her own, as well as the memory of one that still existed in her mind.

Stringing her fingers, she felt the melody in her body and listened to the sound of the voice in her head, her mother's, never forgetting the matter of which she had died, sacrificing herself for a cause: her daughter's life.

Franzie Kane had been shot and killed in the chase that had ensued during the search for a killer who had worked hand in hand with her. She had found the good in her just as her just enough to stop the criminal in his tracks. The fact that she betrayed him was enough to drive him away and he got lost in the crowd and the Lake

Superior Zoo where it took place, ending up in the lion preserve where he was mauled to death.

The song ended and Iris cut the phone off. She sighed, setting her instrument down as she looked at the time on the alarm clock. It was already after noon. Her aunt would be back soon, and she would be having to get dinner ready. Ever since coming to live with her in the midst of the last case, she had gotten around to taking care of things around the house.

Walking downstairs, she grabbed a glass and filled it with water, sipping it as she leaned against the counter, tapping her foot against the floor while thinking about the life she had now, and the love she held for her family. The only remaining family she had.

Her mother would have appreciated this.

Her mother was the one who had made it all possible for her to exist.

Hearing the sound of the car pulling up outside, Iris set the glass down on the counter. A moment later the door opened and her aunt walked in followed by her partner. They looked tired.

"Hey," Iris said.

"You're awake," Diamond said, surprised.

"Yeah. I found it hard to sleep in," she added, "I guess it's just the things running through my head that are troubling me." She embraced her aunt tightly. "I missed you."

Diamond smiled, patting her back. "I've only been gone a day."

Iris closed her eyes, breathing a sigh. "Feels like a long time." She breathed in her aunt's smell. It was a comforting scent, something as sweet as honey and pine.

Diamond looked at Jayson who nodded, walking into the dining room.

Iris released her and walked into the kitchen, grabbing her glass of water. She looked at the clock. It was almost three. Two more hours and she'd start cooking. She heard her aunt talking to her partner in the dining room and listened to how sharp their voices sounded. How distinctly intent they were focused.

Tuning them out, she felt it wasn't her business. Looking in the fridge, she thought of what to cook for supper.

For now, she would find something to take her mind off the past.

IV |

The second body was situated along the beach of Park Point. In the sand, the face pointed skyward, the eyes staring at the sky, as the body remained poised to the killer's effect. The single bullet wound in the temple had ended the man's life and he was growing as cold as the night.

Standing in the sand, the murderer gazed at the waters of Lake Superior, rushing in to wash the shores of the beach. The smells of fresh air and the coming of a rain storm threatening to destroy evidence was all he recognized and as he smiled, cradling his gun in hand, he recalled being here, many years ago, only younger, and the images of his life remained at peace.

For now.

Leaving in the direction towards the walkway that led to the parking lot, he took his car and drove away. The rain began to fall as he crossed the lift bride and he saw the police cars driving past, going in the other direction.

Smiling as he headed into downtown, he curled his fingers on the steering wheel and kept his eyes ahead.

Behind him, the sirens wailed.

Another victim had been found shot to death. Placed anonymously on the beach of Park Point, the police would find it.

The murderer felt a sickening glee as he headed for his residence. The matters which at hand that he'd created were going smoothly. Soon, he would have what he wanted, and there would be no denying his reaction when the target he was after came to him.

Soon, he thought.

The car disappeared with the traffic merging into East Side and then London Road.

By the time the two detectives arrived on scene, the rain had washed away the evidence. The killer was nowhere to be found.

His plan had worked.

| THREE DAYS LATER |

| SUNDAY |

V |

Diamond Kane rested in bed, staring at the ceiling. Beside her, Jayson Bryant had his arm around her and was gently smoothing his hand against her shoulder, while they both wondered what to do about the mysterious ghost killer that was terrorizing the city.

"So," Bryant said, breaking the silence, "what do you think it could be?"

Diamond sighed. "You mean who?" she shook her head. "I don't know."

He shrugged. "Maybe it's just someone with a loose trigger finger. Wanting to kill for the fun of it."

"It's not sport, Jayson. It's murder. People kill at random, I know, but I don't agree with it being fun."

Bryant stared at the ceiling in silence, not replying. Diamond took his hand, staring at his fingers and gently kissing each tip, curled hers through his own. "I want to stop this before it gets out of hand," she said.

"It already is," Bryant said.

Diamond looked at the clock and then seeing the time slowly sat up. "We should get back to the investigation," she said. "See what we can find out about the victims. Their backgrounds."

Bryant said, "I already found out one."

Diamond looked at him. "Who?"

"The man. He was a retired officer who worked on the force back when Lieutenant Sheppard was still a cop."

"What about the woman?"

"She's a citizen. Random killing."

Diamond bit her lip, thinking. "We should talk to Sheppard," she said. "See what he can tell us."

Leaving the bedroom, the two detectives got dressed to leave.

Outside, the weather remained gray and bleak.

Another storm was coming.

VI |

The night had fallen to cover the city and the offices of the department were filled with cops and detectives, secretaries, and working people getting the hour by with paperwork. As Lieutenant Sheppard finished sorting out his judgment on the last victim, he left his office, locking up. He told his secretary he wasn't feeling well and as he walked through the exit to the parking lot, he got to his car and climbing behind the wheel, turned the key, buckling his seatbelt.

The press of something solid touching the back of his neck followed by the sound of a familiar click of round in chamber made him rigid.

"Lieutenant Dawson Sheppard," the voice said, breathing in his ear.

Sheppard forced himself to stay calm as he gripped the wheel with one hand, reaching elsewhere with his second. The gun pressed harder into his neck and he winced.

"Ah, ah, ah," the man said. "Give it." A gloved hand reached forward, outstretched. Sheppard took the weapon from his holster and handed it to the man behind him. He heard him chuckle before the discernible sound of a smile in his voice as he talked.

"You don't remember me, do you?"

Sheppard looked in the rearview mirror. As the figure loomed in the backseat, in the pitch darkness, he furrowed his brow, squinting.

"Who are you?" he said.

Out of the darkness, the form of a face materialized, grinning. The features were pale white, with brown eyes. The hair, a dark color, that was once blonde.

Sheppard stared.

"Officer Sheppard," the boy from his past said, "you killed the man who murdered my parents. The court system failed to prove he was guilty before that happened."

Sheppard heard the tone in the man's voice. He knew what was going to happen.

The gun pressed deeper into his neck as the words filled his ears. The dark brown eyes remained burning as the victimized boy turned homicidal man spoke.

"You are a criminal, Lieutenant. You will pay for your crimes. Now drive."

| MONDAY |

VII |

The lieutenant had been missing for the past eight hours and there was no sign of where he had gone. As the department set out a search party, Sheppard's wife called in to check and see if anyone had heard anything. When Diamond picked up the phone she answered truthfully: no one had heard anything so far.

"I'm so worried," Cora Sheppard said. "He's never like this. If he goes off somewhere he usually calls."

"I promise you," Diamond said. "If we hear anything, we will let you know."

"Thank you, Detective."

Diamond hesitated. Then she asked, "Was there anything you can tell me that might help? Anything that might mean someone would hurt him? Anything from his past?"

Cora thought for a second. Then, as she replied, her voice was filled with uncertainty and dread.

"There was one incident," she said. "A crime he investigated back when he was still a cop. There was a child and he lost both his parents in a shooting." She fell silent before speaking again, her voice raised in pitch. "It couldn't be possible that..." It trailed off.

"That what, Cora?" Diamond said. "What is it?"

"The little boy was adopted by another family and Dawson swore to him that he would make everything right. The next thing I knew after the criminal was let go against everything that he held to be right in justice, the man was found shot dead in his home."

Diamond watched the clock tick away on the wall. She wondered how long it had been since Sheppard had gone missing. After a pause, she spoke:

"All right, Cora," she said. "We'll look into it."

"I'm worried it's him," Cora said. "That it's the boy come back to get my husband all because of the case more than twenty years ago." She added, "Dawson is an innocent man. He doesn't kill innocent people."

Diamond closed her eyes.

"I know," she said.

It was all she could think of to answer.

VIII |

Sheppard's car was found sitting on Midway Road during a routine search of the area. As soon as it was checked, it was clear that the driver had left clean.

There was no blood to be found.

| TUESDAY |

IX |

Evidence found on the old case was discovered by Bryant who showed it to Diamond. They looked over the pictures to see what they could find and seeing the image of a frightened blonde boy with big, teary brown eyes, Diamond felt a sadness and longing to comfort the soul who was no longer that age, but older. She knew that it could be possible a young, innocent soul could turn dark. She had heard of it happening before.

Now it was only a matter of time before they faced it if it was so.

Looking at the name on the file, Diamond read: Chester Grace. The adoption papers stated he had been given the last name Clawson.

"Judging by his birthday, this guy's gotta be almost thirty," Bryant said.

"Good math work," Diamond said. She ran her finger along the page. "The address listed for the house that his parents' were murdered is still standing." She wrote it down on a piece of paper. "My guess is that's where he would be."

Hopefully, she thought, *that's where Sheppard is.*

Leaving the department, the two detectives headed for the lot and as Diamond drove them towards East Side, the traffic flow thickened and time stood still. Her mind thought over the matter of which Cora had told her Sheppard's past.

If the criminal were someone who knew him personally, it was a different matter entirely.

For Sheppard, the matter was personal.

Diamond drove on, challenging red lights.

If he was still alive.

The car ahead stepped on its brakes and Diamond eased on her own. In the distance, the shadows of misfortune laughed.

Someone was going to die.

X |

The living room was dimly lit by a bulb from the ceiling and the smell of cleaning material heavy in the air. As Sheppard stared around him at the familiar place which had not changed one bit since the murder over twenty years ago, he found the vacancy to be disturbing.

"You feel at home?" the man said, staring at him coldly. "Comfortable? Cozy?"

"Chester," Sheppard said. "You don't have to do this. If you turn yourself in—"

The lieutenant stumbled as he felt a sharp pain in the back of his neck and his head spun. The man had struck him from behind, silencing him.

"There's no escape from this life, old man," Chester Clawson said. "You know that as well as I do. The only way out is death." He aimed his gun at the head of the former cop. "Now stay still and *shut up*."

Sheppard winced at the pain in his back and got onto his hands and knees.

"They're coming for me," he said. He turned and saw the look of confidence on the man's face. It was what caused him to regret his decision in having ever involved himself in this.

"I'm counting on it," Clawson said. Keeping an eye towards the door, he kept the gun trained on Sheppard.

Patiently he waited.

Impatiently, fate did not.

XI |

Detective Diamond Kane pulled into the alley behind the house that had been the home for Chester Clawson as a child. Inside she saw the light in the living room and the form of the man standing in its center.

"There he is," Bryant said.

"You take the front," she said. "I'll take the back."

Bryant pulled out his gun and nodded, moving towards the stairs. As he reached the railing he looked around the corner to see Diamond already behind the house.

Taking a breath, he ascended the steps.

XII |

Diamond moved around the back of the house, reaching the door that was unlocked and to her surprise, open. Through the screen she could see the kitchen, empty and dark and as she went in, keeping to the corner, she heard the voices in the living room, the weak one she recognized as her boss.

"You won't win," Sheppard said.

Clawson chuckled darkly. "I already have."

Diamond moved to the hallway and the step leading past the stairs. As she reached the hallway she saw the door leading into the living room vacant and staring at the front of the house, saw the shadow of Bryant on the steps.

"They're still coming for me," Sheppard said.

Clawson's face remained clear of emotion.

"They'll be here soon enough."

Diamond held her gun poised to shoot. Just then the front door burst open. After that everything was a blur.

XIII |

Chester Clawson saw the door burst open, Bryant bursting through with his gun pointed at his chest. Instantly a scowl formed on his face and he raised his gun to shoot. He didn't account for the man on the floor weighing him down.

Sheppard grabbed Clawson's arms and the gun struggled to rise in his grip. As Clawson fought, he tore the weapon from the lieutenant's grip and aimed it at his face.

"You've caused me enough strife," he hissed. "Time to die."

Diamond saw her window closing fast. As she pointed her gun at the arm of the assailant, she pulled the trigger and heard the weapon click. Her eyes widened and she saw the look on Clawson's face form a leer of defiance.

From the front door, Bryant pulled the trigger and the round struck the man in the forehead sending him sprawling him backward as he fell to the floor. His gun slid from nerveless fingers, landing a few feet from his body.

Staring wide eyed at the ceiling, Chester Clawson was dead.

Diamond helped her boss stand, both of them staring at the man's corpse. After over twenty years, it was finally over.

"My gun jammed," she said.

"You should get that checked," he said.

They both laughed. It was a joke that they would always remember and never forget as a near death experience for them all.

Lieutenant Sheppard returned home to his wife while Detective Kane and Detective Bryant went home to Iris. The lives they led were of importance to each other and with another case closed, the fear gone, and the people of the city safe for now, there would be no concern to hold them apart.

Until another time.

| *Years Later*

Blackout. Streets gone dark. That was how he liked it. Everything the way he remembered from a past he could not forget. Existing because he made it. As he looked at the shadows he saw his friends. A memory that would not be forgotten and the likeness of which he would not let go.

Standing on the corner, he watched the life go by, feeling the matter of his own existence remain the same and feeling the potential lift, thoughts of suicide, becoming him. He wanted to die. He wanted to know what it was like to feel the slow blade cutting his wrists and tempting to see the blood, the bluish veins as they opened to reveal every part of him from the other side.

Then he would be with his friends.

Watching the girl as she walked the avenue in the dark, he paced himself, preparing for what it took to take the next step, following the steps she took and as he made it to the spot where she had once stood, he stopped, seeing her staring at him as she turned around, facing the black.

"Hello?"

Her voice, revealing fright. Fear. Sudden temptation that meant she was scared. As she saw him, but did not notice him the night, she continued to walk forward.

Slowly, his footsteps matched with her own. Her breathing was his own. Her heart beat was his to own. He came closer and closer still.

He was upon her.

Gripping her with his hand clamped over her mouth he felt her fighting him, her body taut, a loaded spring.

Quickly, he drew the blade over her throat.

The spring snapped, becoming limp. The eyes bulged in the head as the girl became suddenly limp. He released her and looked around. No one was to see him.

Only his friends recognized his pain.

Looking at her again, he saw her form against the ground and felt a rain drop strike him. The sound of thunder echoed in the distance.

He smiled.

His friends would wash away the evidence.

Taking the blade, he slowly drew it across his cheek, drawing fresh blood. It dripped down the handle, covering his hand. As he knelt down, he touched the girl's lifeless face, her lips. The same hand covered in blood left evidence.

It would not be gone by morning.

| Thursday |

XIV |

Detective Diamond Kane clutched the evidence bag, staring at the clothing inside, what remained of the girl's bodily covering. She shook her head, seeing the body, laying naked upon the ground.

Torture, she thought. It was harm to one's eyes. Everyday to see the damage done to humanity by heartless men and women who beat and bruised as well as stole the lives of innocent people. There was nothing she could do but watch the matter resolve itself.

Justice.

A cruel deal in the world of the department she involved herself in.

"Detective," a cop said, walking over. "We found something."

Diamond nodded as the man came up, his hands hugging his body against the frost. "Show me," she said. She was led back to the body. Back to the crime. As they reached the form of the girl, the cop crouched, directing a finger to the face.

"The lips," the cop said. "We found fingerprint residue and blood."

"He touched her," she said.

"There's just one thing," the officer said. "It's not her blood."

Diamond frowned, waiting for the resolve.

"We think it might be his."

A careless killer. One I'm searching for in the winter. Again, Diamond found her heart in the right place. This girl's death would be brought to justice.

Facing the street, she looked at the avenue and the bare curbs without streetlights.

"He knew where to strike," she said. "He knew there would be no chance she would spot him."

"Careful," the cop said, "not careless."

"Good work." Diamond smiled. "I'll give word to the lieutenant to have you given a higher standard."

The man waved his hand. "It's what I do every day, Detective. I got nothing to show for myself but this job. It's all I have besides my family. Wife, kids." He nodded. "You do what you have to."

She watched him head for his cruiser. Letting out a sigh she turned back to the body and shaking her head, saw the cruel work done.

He slit her throat, she thought, *from behind. Then he touched her with his own blood.*

On the lips.

A message.

Diamond felt a chill and it wasn't the cold.

He wasn't killing for fun.

It was a fetish.

XV |

Seated at her desk, Diamond typed away at her laptop, making the first report final. She shook her head, tucking a loose strand of hair from her eyes as she saw the words flowing onto the screen. She wanted them to make sense and there was no other way better to make the sensible truth understood than to clarify what she thought about the killer.

Finishing the final paragraph, she stared at the words and taking a deep breath, tapped enter to send it in, closing the computer and grabbing her coat, left the office, heading for her car as she left the building.

She found that as she drove to the mall, trying to get her mind off the factor of death that she was thinking about Franzie and how her sister's sacrifice to save her in the end had been one that shook her world as well as her niece's, there had been no telling what could be done about the fact of them both shaping out to become what Franzie feared and after the killer ended up in the lion's den at the zoo—literally—the case was closed and Diamond found herself more separated from family.

The cases came in, the years passed. Time wore her. She became older and she felt the creases of life opening to let her leak unwanted sorrows.

Parking in the Food Court parking lot, she felt her eyes burning and leaning over the steering wheel, let the sadness flow.

After nearly ten years of holding it in, it felt somewhat good to let the pain out.

XVI |

He sat in the darkness of the room, his shirt off. As he held the blade poised in his hand, he gripped it tightly, watching the light catching silver. His eyes saw the poison. His medicine.

He wanted it. He wanted to taste it.

Closing his eyes, he saw the darkness behind them. As he guided the blade to his right arm, he pressed the point against the veins of his wrist, feeling the edge dig in.

Slowly, he pressed harder.

Edge broke vein.

He felt a sudden flash of agony before control.

Drawing the knife up, he opened his eyes which were tear filled and saw the ceiling above spinning with lights.

"For you," he said out loud.

Finally, with the same hand, he brought the blade to his neck and as the sirens filled his ears, he sliced deep and hard.

Without noise the world faded.

He saw nothing but darkness after that.

| One Month Later |

XVII |

The city of Duluth was still at peace. Everyone felt as safe as they had before, as if the reckoning of danger was now over. People went on about their lives, parents hugged their children goodbye as they went to school.

Life went on.

If not for one person.

XVIII |

Standing before the grave, Diamond Kane was dressed in black, clutching a red rose by its stem. She looked upon the granite and saw the look of the freshly planted headstone that was to mark the final resting place. Standing beside her, Iris Kane held her aunt's arm and watched her reconcile with what was on her mind.

"I still don't know why he turned," Diamond said. "I just can't find a reason to believe he was wrong." Her niece rubbed her back. She sighed.

"It's not your fault," Iris said. "He made his way. He chose his path."

Diamond's lip trembled and she shook her head. "I just can't believe he'd do it." Her voice broke and Iris embraced her, holding her while she sobbed.

On the tombstone, before her, it read:

HERE LIES

JAYSON BRYANT

FRIEND AND ALLY

MAY HIS SPIRIT REST IN HEAVEN

| bonus story

Here's one originally published by itself; I would rather have it as a bonus to read.

Please enjoy: *Act of Measure.*

Note, I used the same name twice (accident lol).

Act of Measure

Prologue |

August 1979

The strobe lights of police cars lit up the block, the sound of ambulance sirens in the distance echoing back to the ears of the kid who was seated in the back of the cruiser parked side-by-side with his mother's Pontiac Trans Am.

His mother was dead.

"You got what you wanted now give me the name, your stupid sumbitch," the cop jerked the man from where he sat on the curb, grabbing him by the collar of his shirt and bringing him forward, hauled him close enough to smell the alcohol on his breath. "When the shot was fired who pulled the trigger? Who was it? Who had the gun, dammit?!"

The man cocked his head, staring with fogged eyes and a drooling mouth. He said, "I can't remember officer. It's all gone from my mind."

The cop grew red faced. He breathed heavily through his nose, his breath fogging the air and the perspiration festered on his upper lip. Reaching for the Colt 45 at his hip he was going to pull it out and draw the trigger to make this bum-drunk-happy mother-fucker face his day when the boy spoke up.

"Dad, stop," the kid's voice was strong, his tone calm. Yet still it carried an edge that was somehow meaningful. He stood from the cruiser and walked to where the two men stood at odds with one another by the curb. Turning to glance at the Pontiac Trans Am, he saw the shattered windshield and the driver's seat beyond, caked in blood. He could almost read the patterned display in which his mother's blood had made a painted picture in the coupe.

"Go back to the car," his father's voice, commanding and hopeful that he would listen. When he didn't move, his father said it firmly. "Lincoln, get back in the car, *now*. Right now. I mean it." He watched his son stare at him open eyed and without emotion. His feelings were no longer of any age to be consented. He was now a broken-hearted child without a mother who would never be able to see him grow up, or to see him graduate and have grandkids and grow old as grandparents before death came knocking at the front door.

The kid walked closer to the two men. He looked the drunk in the eye, and he said, "Tell me who pulled the trigger. You know who did it. Tell me, and I'll have my father go easy on you, just enough so that maybe you'll be breathing when you get to the courthouse."

The father blinked, but remained still, holding his posture. The drunk looked from the man, then to the kid and then back to the man. His lower lip began to tremble, and he uttered a sob.

"All right," he whined, "all right, man. I'll tell you. It was . . . Moriarty."

"You son of a bitch!"

The yell came from across the street. All three of their heads turned. A shot rang out in the dark, followed by a ribbon of blood bursting like a flower on the drunk's shirt. The cop and the boy stumbled back and away from each other, the boy grabbing for his father's belt at the same time. Running at them from the avenue, a man had his gun drawn, aimed at the cop and was stalking towards the Pontiac. Whatever reason there was behind his madness was gone. He was now clinically insane.

The cop reached to his belt, struggling to find the Colt and as his fingers grasped nothing, he turned his head, toward his son. The boy held the weapon in his hand, arms outstretched, trained on the man barreling towards them.

"Lincoln, no!"

Three shots echoed in tandem, each sounding like thunderclaps in the rain drenched darkness. The man's legs buckled, and his gun slid from nerveless fingers, hitting the pavement before sliding across gravel underneath the coupe. The boy watched as he came to rest within a few feet of where he stood, and then seeing the chance to react, he crouched, keeping the gun trained on the now dying assailant. He inhaled the air, which tasted of rain, the moisture touching his lips, covering his cheeks in a film. He watched the man before him on the ground as he breathed his last breath, his chest filling with blood, he knew, from the bullets that had entered his lungs.

"Lincoln," his father said. "Give me the gun."

The boy didn't hear him. He was still staring at the man, seeing the life being drained across the pavement in a pool of red. Watching the glint of silver pinned on his chest, flash in the sudden blaze of lightning.

A badge.

"Son."

The boy turned to his father. He looked at him and saw the meaningfulness in his eyes. Then, as he let it drop to his side, he handed the piece over to him and allowed his father to be take him into the welcoming arms of someone he could trust, and the only family he had left. For the future held a better present, and besides, he thought, the worst part would be over.

For now.

| Part One |

I |

Thirty-Three Years Later

The blade rested at the foot of the dead man seated, bleeding out in the chair. His throat was slit, and his eyes remained wide, staring blank at the ceiling. His face was slack, his mouth agape, as if making a final protest. It was not in his past nature. Everything he had done, and everything he could have to stop what was about to from happening was now impossible.

Crossing the dining room to the living room floor, the killer took careful steps, making his way into the hall and wasted no time in glancing upon the pictures that hung on the wall of the family the man had in his life. He kept going, farther, towards the door near the kitchen, and stopped, then with a gloved hand twisted the knob, turning it clockwise. Hearing the discernible click as the latch was locked, he cursed his luck, and listened to the distant sound of sirens coming down the street. Stealing a glance through the kitchen he saw the sliding doors that led onto an open deck and patio. Stealing a glance at his watch, he checked the time. There was no chance to get the item he required from the basement.

The cops busted in through the front door. Behind them, a man strode in, dressed in a trench coat and dark navy suit with a white tie. His hair was slicked back and brown, and his eyes, a cold hazel, searched the room for sign of where the crime was, or had been. Seeing the victim, the man in the chair, his throat cut from ear to ear and the knife near his feet, the detective grimaced, turning back and muttering a curse.

"God, there goes my dessert," an officer said, stepping back out of the house.

"Hold it together."

"Easy for you to say."

The detective, Lincoln Sebastian, met the younger man's eyes. Although only apart by four years, Sebastian felt superiority over him.

"Nothing's easy," he said and nodded to the door. "Get in there. Hold your stomach, dammit. Make sure you find *something*."

The cop took one look through the door and then nodded. "You got it." He stepped in. Sebastian watched him go, without a word in response. As he mustered the patience of a thousand judges, hoping and praying that something could be found, he watched from the top of the stairs, staring at the sky for a moment, for a tell if the rain would wash away any evidence that was to be found. The graying clouds overhead told a different story and it was the very nightmare that every technician feared.

Sebastian felt a drop strike his neck and sighed. Turning back to the house he looked inside and as he saw the team scouting each room, finding nothing, knew that it was useless. As he walked in, towards the kitchen, he stopped, turning to look at the basement door. Reaching into his pocket, he pulled on a glove, and turning the knob, felt the restrain.

Locked.

Frowning, he went back to the living room and to the man seated in the chair. His face was to the ceiling, looking towards the heavens in a hope that it was where he was headed. As he gingerly picked through the pockets of his coat, he felt something in the left jeans pocket and hearing a jingle, pulled out a row of keys.

"Bingo."

Walking back to the door, Sebastian was careful not to smudge the lock with the blood from his palm. As he tried each key, he was shocked to find that the first seven didn't work.

The eighth however, slid into the lock with ease. Saying a prayer, he turned the key. The lock snapped. Turning the knob, he felt the door budge and then pulling it open towards the outer wall, smelled the odor of old wood and stone. Seeing darkness beyond the threshold, he reached out, finding a light switch and flicking it, heard a bulb buzzing downstairs as a yellow glow inhabited the black. Descending carefully, he was wary of the last two steps as they seemed to be weakened with age.

The basement was separated into two areas. To his right, was a mudroom, with an array of shoes, as well as clothes and a few boxes. To his left, a washer and dryer and a back area for a sink basin that was yellowed with grime. The smell of disinfectant and the odor of a stronger stench, one more than foul, assailed his nostrils. He ignored it, walking toward the mudroom. As he reached the first row of boxes, he spotted something within the mess, that was neater among the rest: a black suitcase, fashioned with a silver combination lock and a gold handle.

Furrowing his brow, he reached out, and using his fingers, carried the case to the dryer, setting it on top. That was when he saw the initials on the handle: SD. Shaking his head, Sebastian pondered what this meant.

"Detective?"

"Yeah?"

"He's gone."

Sebastian sighed. After a moment he returned upstairs, heading outside with the case. He set it on the hood of his Volvo sedan and removed the glove, pocketing it. Staring at his watch he wondered what to do next. Looking up at the house he waited for the crew to be finished and then got behind the wheel, setting the case in the seat beside him.

SD.

He was going to find out who the initials belonged to.

II |

His fingers trembled as he dialed each key. The number formed on the pad and then, as he pressed TALK, he listened for the dial tone, hearing the beep before connection. The following silence was still, and unnerving. He swallowed dryly, wishing he had a cup of water, something to quench his thirst. As he stared at the writing upon the pad sitting on his desk, he knew it was only a matter between him and the person on the other line that kept him in place.

Sean Miller recognized his fate as soon as it was sealed.

The Verso Corporation plant down the service road Recycle Way, housed his office. He had been working as assistant manager for the past year and gained successful employment. The records showed that he was a trustworthy employee and would never fail to succeed over his other peers. The man in charge, Ryan Rayburn, had claimed he was just as trustworthy and could be relied upon for everything.

Everything, that was, except for keeping the statements clean.

Before the past three months, Sean Miller had been living a good life—hell, a great life—he had a wife he loved, a job he enjoyed working, and a car he loved to drive. The salary he gained from the line of work he was employed kept him on his toes. He budgeted each two-week check accordingly, and as he spent his money, he kept in mind that one day, something would come along, something good, or bad, that he would have to face and it was going to be either his line of work on the line, or his wife's life that mattered.

As Christmas came and went, the holidays were joyous, cheerful almost. As Miller accepted the fact that he was incapable of making children, that his loins were not to spawn, he realized his life was not all that he wanted it to be. He sat at his desk that evening, drinking straight from a bottle of Jack Daniels that came from the office party, and listened to the sound of bustling work and pages being shifted, and forklifts, and steamrollers, he felt he didn't want this life anymore.

Digging in the top drawer of his desk, he found the 22. Caliber weapon and checking to make sure that bullets were in the chamber, he looked at his watch, seeing the time. It was only an hour until midnight. Sixty minutes until the new year. He closed his eyes, pressing the weapon into his mouth, tasting the flavor of steel.

The phone rang.

Miller opened his eyes. He looked at the receiver in its cradle. Looking at his watch he frowned, the gun still in his mouth. Looking past the windows at the floor outside he saw no one, not even the janitor, just empty space.

The phone rang a second time.

Laying the gun on the desk, Miller reached for the receiver, picking up the cursed instrument and then placing it to his ear, answered.

"Hello?"

"Mr. Miller," a voice said, sounding collect, measured. "I wonder how you are this very moment. Hopefully you aren't thinking about pulling that trigger. I'm certain that your wife would not be happy if she found out you killed yourself before thinking about adoption."

Looking back through the windows that viewed the floor and the cubicles, Miller felt a sudden curiosity and a sliver of fear. He wondered who this person was. He also wondered how he knew what he was doing.

"Who are you?" he asked. "What do you want? I have a right to know."

The voice chuckled. "Oh, Mr. Miller, don't we all?" there was a pause and then the man said, "I think that you could be of greater use to someone like me. Your job is somewhat of a drag, I understand, and being you can't procreate a child, which is a shame, believe me, I think that I can help you."

Miller squinted at the desk, looking at the gun. He felt a steadiness, feeling ready to comply to anything. The phone call had been sudden. A wonder he was even capable of making the wise decision to listen.

"How can I do that?"

"Let's just say, it's a bargain. I pay you whatever I feel is the proper price and is above your pay grade and you do something for me." He shook his head. "Let's start with a simple job."

Now, holding the receiver to his ear, and knowing that he had screwed up, that he had failed the mysterious caller, Miller listened to the line ring. As it rang three times, he heard the other side pick-up, followed by a clear voice asking, "You did the job?"

He fought the panic as he knew the dread was going to make him sound even more like a liar. Looking at the desk, he said, "I couldn't get the item you requested."

A sigh breathed heavily into the phone. "I told you, Mr. Miller. You were either in or out."

"I swear, I tried."

"Trying doesn't cut it. I needed that item. You failed me. Consider our allegiance terminated."

"Wait—"

Click.

Miller's hand shook as he returned the phone to its cradle. Biting his bottom lip, he stood, pushing back the swivel chair and walking to the door of the office, peered out at the floor. He saw no one, only empty seats and computer screens. Returning to his chair, he pulled out a key and digging out the file he wanted, tucked it underneath his arm, leaving the office and locking the door behind him, strode to the stairs that led to the main work floor.

"Headed out for the day, Mr. Miller?" a worker called as he manned a steam roller, driving it over a roll of product that was to become the next batch of used pages. Miller stared at the man. "Yeah, I think I'm done," he said and turning away, walked outside, the cool night air chilling him as he glanced to the right and then the left, seeing the bushes and grass, the still remaining leaves from fall as they scraped the gravel. Looking at his watch he shook his head, ignoring the feeling of dread. He got behind the wheel of his Cadillac CTS and inhaled the scent of the interior. As he wrinkled his nose, wondering what the smell was, he couldn't place it. Sliding the key into the ignition he turned it.

The Cadillac CTS exploded in a fireball, the noise of the car bomb bringing the attention of the workers and they scrambled to investigate, finding the assistant manager's vehicle in flames. There was no saving him as the last thought going through Sean Miller's mind had been that he recognized the strange odor.

It was burnt toast.

III |

Sebastian handed cash over to the clerk behind the desk and the man stared at the fold of hundreds. He looked up at Sebastian and blinked.

"I only carry bills for transfers," the detective said, giving him a reassuring smile. "It's for the Audi. I'm trading in my 1998 Volvo S70."

The kid, dressed in ragged blue jeans and a faded red business shirt with a cap that covered his bleached blonde hair, stared at the man for a moment before he gave a slow nod. "Right," he said. "I'll just have you sign the papers and then give you the keys. The tank should be filled already."

"It's no problem. I'm making a gas station run before I go to work."

"What business are you in?"

"I'm a cop," Sebastian said. "Detective, actually. I solve cases. Investigations that have grown cold or happen in the area."

The kid nodded again, still holding the money in his hands. "Sounds intense."

The gong of Big Ben could be heard from Sebastian's pocket and he fished the cell phone out of his coat, staring at the ID before he looked at the kid and said, "I need to take this." Turning back to look outside he saw the overcast of darkness and the night that was falling over Duluth. Clearing his throat, he answered, "This is Sebastian."

"Sebastian this is Lieutenant Wayne Lovejoy." His boss's voice carried over the line cheerfully, yet with something in mind which he knew could only mean there was something serious he needed a favor for. "I'm calling to inform you we have another death on our hands. It appears the assistant manager of Verso Company was car bombed outside his office this afternoon. Sean Miller was the victim. I want you to go over the crime scene, see what you can find then get back to me."

Sebastian turned back to see the kid behind the desk counting the money, dolling out pay that would go towards the car and as he shifted his gaze to the view outside, seeing the clouds gathering to make rain, he allowed himself to take in the fact that it wasn't going to be an evening he could rest without finding strife at his back door. It never was. Even if the body was taken care of and the family notified, there was still the paperwork and the management to investigate.

"I'll be there," he said.

"Good, I knew I could count on you. I'll be expecting your call."

Sebastian slid the phone back into his pocket. Turning he saw that the kid had the keys and was holding them out.

"I can handle the rest, Detective," he said. "You can take the car. The money covers it." He smiled nervously. "Good luck on your case."

Sebastian looked the kid over. He was somewhere between nerd and punk. Pursing his lips, he sighed. "Thanks." Heading outside he smelled the odor of rain and tasted it on the air. He breathed in the aroma of the coming storm and strode quickly across the lawn, passing between cars before reaching the midnight black, Audi A6. He pressed the remote to unlock it and heard the beep of the horn. Climbing in he smelled the scent of cleaned interior along with the aroma of car freshener. As he turned the key in the ignition, he shut the door and buckled his seat belt, feeling the cool air of the vents blow on his face. Shutting the air conditioner off and checking the gas gauge, he saw it was a full tank.

There was no need to make a gas station run after all.

The hotel room was dimly lit by a single bulb within the lamp shade. As the flickering sign outside glowed, the smell of cigarettes and mildewed carpet assailed the nostrils of the man seated in the chair beside the bed. Resting over the sheets, dressed only in her undergarments with her wrists and ankles bound, the woman was quiet. Her eyes on the ceiling, she wept, fearing the moment that would come next. She had begun to wonder what had happened to her husband and feeling the dread that he was dead, she cried, understanding it was she who was next.

The man smiled, touching the gun to his knee and tapping it, made the sound of steel against metal. "It's funny," he said. "I lost this when I was only twelve. Horse riding accident. Thing bucked me off and I landed fifteen feet away. The doctor who did the surgery fucked it up and about a year later it broke in two." The stranger paused, his voice on edge. "He said he was sorry." He chuckled, staring at the woman now, seeing the fear in her eyes. "You know your husband never said sorry. Not once. He never apologized to me at all. He just said he couldn't do it. Couldn't get what I needed and that just makes me *mad*."

The woman's eyes widened as she watched the suppressor being screwed to the barrel. The gun was aimed at her temple and pressed there, hard. She felt the cold of the gun and whimpered.

"*Shut—up—bitch.*" The man glowered, narrowing his eyes. "You're worth more trouble to me alive than dead. I should just kill you." He pressed the gun harder into her temple. So hard in fact that the woman felt her neck pop. She squealed in agony and then he stopped, releasing her. He snickered, chuckling wildly. "I just want this all to end, you know . . . I just want it to *stop*." He laughed and sat back in the chair, staring at the gun in his hand. He looked at the silencer and then pressing the edge to his forehead felt the gap between life and death. "I just feel so close. So close to being with him," his voice was soft. "I just want that day to come where I can finally be at peace. Away from the pain and the suffering . . . you know. Where all this can *end*." He drooled as he eased his finger on the trigger, closing his eyes. Then, as they opened, his face turned, looking to the woman. She stared at him, wincing at the pain as she felt her vertebrae tighten with the knot in her spine.

Suddenly, he turned away, mingling with darkness. When she stared into the shadows, she saw nothing but the flashing light of the hotel sign.

The strange man had gone, leaving her tied to the bed.

IV |

Detective Lincoln Sebastian stood outside the maintenance doors of the Verso Company building and watched the steamrollers, the workers beyond and above in offices filing papers—all noise and sound that drowned out his thoughts on the fact: the assistant manager, Sean Miller was dead. His car had been rigged to blow with a bomb that ignited with a set of tubes running from the ignition to the gas tank. The moment Miller turned the key the click of the motor caused a chain reaction that caused the Cadillac CTS to become a raging inferno. The assistant manager's final resting place of hell.

"Detective," a technician waved to him. Sebastian walked over to the car, once having shined with the gleam of a luxury sedan, now a charred carriage that had carried its occupant from this world into the next. "The body was burnt beyond recognition; the guy died instantly."

The detective stared at the kid. "I know that," he said, shoving his hands in his coat pockets. Raising his brow, he inquired, "Got anything else?"

The tech swallowed nervously. "Um, yeah." Reacting quickly to what it was he had to show, he turned back to his kit. Withdrawing an evidence bag, he passed it to Sebastian who eyed the charred remains of what was inside. "Check it out. It was in the passenger's seat. Got caught up in the flames, but I think we can get some ink off at the lab."

"It's a file," Sebastian said, eying the curled edges of what had been a folder containing documents. He saw the red ink, faded, and blinked as he felt a sudden drop of rain. Looking up he saw the clouds still gray and then turning to the tech, handed the evidence back to him. "Do your best. Make sure you find out what this is. I want it by the end of the week."

The kid smiled, feeling reconciliation. "Right away, sir," he said and packed the bag away. Watching the detective walk back to his car and then seeing the red taillights flash as he started the engine, he waited for him to drive out of the lot and turn down Recycle Way before closing the case. Standing from his crouch he walked to the van and tossing the bag in the back, closed the doors. He followed the service road and headed into West Duluth, following narrow streets to the highway. As he passed the WLSSD water treatment plant to his right, he wrinkled his nose, inhaling the odor of rank liquids being cleaned and fertilized for further use. He hated the smell.

Exiting onto 21st Avenue West he followed traffic to the stoplights on Piedmont Avenue. As the lights turned red, he eased on the brake, hearing the wet of gears beneath him screech in protest. Glancing in his rearview mirror, the tech saw the glare of headlights behind him, blinding him with white glare. He blinked and waved to the driver to turn his brights off, but the person obviously didn't see.

The light turned green. He stepped on the gas and the van inched forward slowly. The driver didn't back off, but accelerated, and he turned into the opposite lane, using his turn signal, the person behind him swerving left, beside him. He felt the traction of his tires beginning to lift, rain pouring in a deluge on the windshield and he found the steering wheel unresponsive to steer. Feeling his body react instinctively to the hydroplane, he allowed the vehicle to take control. As he did, he felt the van start to drift, becoming steady, the tires reconnecting with the road.

He felt comfort too soon.

The car beside him, the driver behind the wheel steered, driving their car into the side of the van, and the correction was halted. The tech felt the van spin into a skid before turning sideways and as other cars in the side lane veered to get out of the way, he gripped the wheel to gain control—too late. The weight of the vehicle won, and the automobile lifted off its tires, flipping then rolling, once, twice, and then three times, coming to rest on its tires, albeit by chance, three yards away. The driver of the other vehicle, a black car, pulled to a stop, tires skidding over wet asphalt. The door opened, and a slender woman climbed out. Looking left and then right, she tossed back her head, using her hands to tie her pale blonde hair into a ponytail. Her piercing blue eyes stared at the van while she reached to the holster at her belt, grabbing for the .45 caliber Sig Sauer and sliding her finger beneath the trigger aimed it towards the sky. Pulling it twice she blasted off two rounds, the echo sounding loud in the surrounding air. People fled as others strayed, getting back into their cars and driving away. In the van, the tech remained unconscious.

Heels clicking against the cement, the woman walked the distance, and reaching the door, grabbed the handle, tearing it open, and then pulling the man from his seat after removing his seatbelt, tossed him to the ground. The young man groaned, and she crouched over him, holding the gun aimed at his head.

"Where is it?" she said. "I won't ask again."

The kid opened his eyes. Staring at the gun and then at the woman, he felt a sudden realization that it was useless. With a shaky hand he pointed to the rear door of the van. "There," he said, "in the back."

The woman smiled; her lips thin against a pretty face. "Thank you." Pointing the gun at the younger man's leg, she fired. Hearing him yell in pain she stepped towards the vehicle, ignoring the screams of other people as they watched, still waiting for the cops to arrive. As the sound of sirens grew close, the woman found the contents she was searching for and walking back to the kid, eyed his expression of agony. When he saw that she was considering making him a permanent scar of blood on the pavement he closed his mouth, whimpering, hot tears still flowing from his eyes. She stepped over him and walked back to her car. The black sedan peeled down the avenue and then a side street, passing through a red light. Gripping his leg, the tech felt shock overtake him and the world turned cold.

Closing his eyes, he allowed the memory of his life to fade.

V |

Sebastian stood to the side of the four-lane road, sipping his coffee, watching the tech being loaded on the stretcher. He focused on the fiberglass and tire tracks left behind, what was the trail of the car leaving the scene. The driver had gotten away clean. She—witnesses had said a woman—had tailed the van and as it was veering out of control, the woman had made a move, ramming the vehicle, sending it rolling about three yards away, where it rested on its tires, windshield spiderwebbed but still intact.

Shaking his head, he waited for the next car to pass before crossing and held up his hand with his badge to indicate that he was of importance.

"He's out of it, Detective," the EMT said. "There's not much he can tell you."

Staring at the glassy eyes of the kid, Sebastian watched them gaze towards the sky and then turn to look at him, widening as they focused on his face. Pointing to the van, he asked, "Where is the file, son? Who took it?"

A harsh intake of breath. Like wind through a tunnel, only trapped. The kid's lungs were starting to fail him as shock overtook his system. The medic gave oxygen and the tech breathed, inhaling the fresh, clean air. As the eyes grew more aware and focused, the kid mumbled something. Sebastian leaned over him and placed his ear next to the mask.

"What was that?"

"It's . . . gone. She took it."

The EMTs hurried the stretcher to the back of the waiting ambulance. He waited until the sirens had started to fade into the distance before walking to the van. Glass crunched under foot and he smelled the odor of gasoline as it still leaked from the ruptured tank. Wrinkling his nose, he sipped coffee, went to the rear of the vehicle, finding the evidence bag gone, much like the kid had said and then looking towards the front he turned, walking to the driver's side, peering in over the steering wheel, finding nothing of importance there. He walked across the two lanes to where his car was parked and getting behind the wheel, started the engine, pulling into traffic that was headed towards the mall and feeling his eyes starting to grow heavy, realized how much sleep he'd had in the past two days wasn't enough to fuel him through the evening.

Driving the long route through traffic past Miller Hill Mall and the businesses that thrived in Hermantown, he traveled to Stebner Road and his house. Pulling into the driveway he parked, getting out and tossing the remains of his coffee in the garbage by the garage walked to the front door, sliding the key in the lock before stepping into the cool air of the living room. It was a calming change to the intense aromatic feel of the day.

The house he lived in had been home for the past ten years. He had moved here after his father died of heart failure. The man had judged himself too many drinks and after several years on the job as an officer of the law, he had retired, only to find that the years had caught up with him. He had fought the grip of death until the very end.

Checking the clock on the stove, Sebastian saw it was only ten after eleven. He felt groggy and wondered how much longer he could stand. Walking to the bedroom he sat on the end of the bed and kicking off his shoes, lay on the empty queen-sized mattress that he shared with no one. It had been years since he had found love, let alone trusted himself to be with someone with which he could share his life. Being single was something he enjoyed, and it never bothered him; he had always felt comforted by the silence.

As the hours ticked by, Sebastian's eyes closed, and he drifted to sleep, having dreams that carried into thoughts he wished he could forget.

The heart rate monitor beeped as the technician's pulse was tracked and minutes of his life, sounding the clock of his existence. The silence in the hallway was clear and as the nurse in the station finished signing documents, she closed the binder, setting it back into the cabinet. Looking at her watch she yawned, covering her mouth with her forearm. Grabbing the chart hung on the wall and untucking the pen from her blouse she went on her rounds. She found each patient was in satisfactory condition, save for a few minorities of breathing or bathroom accidents. She exhaled a sigh and hummed a tune as she walked back to the station, slipping the clipboard back on the wall, before returning to her desk. Signing out of the computer and standing up she went on her break.

Several minutes passed before the elevator doors slid open. A figure stepped out, dressed in a janitor's outfit. The man whistled a song that was in his head and pushed his carriage across the floor. The wheels were noiseless as they ran over the carpet before reaching the desk. Behind him, a slender woman with black hair in a nurse's uniform pushing a cart for blood draw walked down the hall, coming to stand by the wall. She looked to see where the nurse had gone. Turning to the man, she watched him check his watch and as soon as he nodded, she grabbed the clipboard, running her finger along the page. Finding the name and room number she set the clipboard back where she'd found it.

"Quickly," the man said and then she reached into the pocket of her uniform, grabbing out a vial of clear liquid. Taking one of the syringes from the cart, she plunged the air from it and then slipping the needle into its top, drew the contents. The liquid filled the syringe and she waited until the vial was empty to look down the hall. Crossing to the room where the tech was asleep, she tested the needle, squirting some back into the vial. Slipping the contents into her uniform, she blinked, wincing at the pain in her eyes. The smell of the poison stung. Looking back, she watched the man beckon for her to hurry and turned. Sliding the needle into the IV line she pressed the plunger down, watching the pressure of contents fill the water that was entering the kid's bloodstream.

As the fire that filled his veins roused him from the quiet rest that was his last, the tech opened his eyes, turning his head to see the recognizable features staring back at him, smiling. Opening his mouth to scream, he felt a hand clamp over his mouth and as the flames in his body found their way to his heart, he whimpered a final time before the darkness came to claim him.

The nurse removed her hand and turned to the janitor, watching him stare at the lifeless body. They knew they had their work done for now.

The two left the floor before the nurse returned to find the dead tech and her panic was enough to make a call to the department. She knew it had been murder. As soon as the tapes were run back and the police arrived, the call was made to Lieutenant Wayne Lovejoy that the kid was dosed with poison.

Standing and staring at the younger man's wide pleading eyes, even as in death, the lieutenant understood the pain the tech had gone through before his demise.

The murderer had used bleach.

VI |

"Yeah, thanks Margaret, I'll get on that as soon as I can."

Placing the phone back in its cradle, Detective Lincoln Sebastian stared at the desk and the case that was placed there. For the longest time he could not figure out what it was or what was inside it. Or, what the initials meant that were carved into the golden handle.

SD.

Still, it made him think about the fact that the victim was not without an heir. The man who had been killed had been identified: Kyle Danes. A prominent lawyer who worked in a firm based in the Cities, it's home office in Seattle, more than two hundred miles South of Duluth. The innocence of Danes' choices had been displayed clearly on his resume—he worked as an advisor for a company and its ties were towards the recent car bomb victim, and assistant manager of Verso Company, Sean Miller.

The two had been somehow connected, but its evaded Sebastian's mind as to what they had been working on. The police had searched the house and Danes' office as thoroughly as possible and found nothing. Not a single scrap. It was then of course that the anonymous tip had been given about a cleaning man that had come in shortly after Danes left his office to go home for the evening and with his cap down low, shielding his features from the camera which went black for only a minute or so before coming back on, he was seen leaving. When the police arrived to check for evidence, they found it was gone.

The cleaning man was nowhere to be found.

The same thing had happened almost similarly at the hospital when the technician in the van accident near Piedmont had been murdered by injecting bleach into his IV line. The nurse was with black hair but seemed oddly familiar to Sebastian as he looked at the sketch given by one of the people who said they saw a blonde female who had the same features as the brunette. The cleaning man had the same build as the one who had raided Danes' Duluth office. The man kept his cap down and shielded his face. There was nothing to tell of his features or who he was.

Shaking his head and rubbing his eyes, Sebastian checked his watch. It was nearing noon. He heard distant thunder rolling in the sky. He knew it was going to rain again. Looking at the case he checked the combination lock and then noted that there were six keys to be turned that would unlock it. Still sitting in his chair, he dug into his top drawer and finding the file on Kyle Danes, fished through the pages, finding the photograph of the lawyer. Beside him in the picture, was his wife, Peyton, who had died a month earlier after suffering a brain hemorrhage while at the dinner table. Between them and in their embrace, the colorful teenager with striped red hair and darkly made up eyes glared into the lens, watching the camera man take the picture. Sebastian stared into the gaze of the child who had no parents, and who was no longer a teen but an adult, having grown to be in a cover band that was playing at Pizza Luce downtown.

Taking the photo and sliding it into his coat, Sebastian slipped the folder back into the desk and leaving his office, headed out of the department to his car, remembering the initials on the case.

SD.

He drove through the torrential downpour, following the streets and finding his way into traffic going through downtown reached the restaurant and bar, parking across the avenue and feeding the meter, ran across the street to the doors. Stepping in, he shook off the wet and taking out the photo, glanced around. People were seated at tables, eating pasta, steak, pizza, burgers, and drinking beer, pop, or water. Some of them turned to stare at him as he walked up to one of the waitresses who inquired, "Can I help you with something?"

Sebastian refrained from showing his badge. He asked, "Is there a band playing here this afternoon?"

The young woman smiled. "Well, yeah," she said, smartly. "It's the entertainment for tonight. You hoping to get laid?"

Some people in the restaurant started to laugh. Sebastian felt himself growing heated. He gave up on decency and reaching for his badge, flashed it to the surrounding crowd. The people silenced immediately. Showing the photograph, he said, "I'm here to see this girl. She's older now, in her late twenties. I'm wondering if her band is playing. Can anyone tell me if they are here or not?"

A man wearing a Nirvana tee shirt and balding with a septum piercing pointed to the door leading to the bar. "She's in there, man," he said and standing, walked over to open the door. Inside, drums could be heard followed by the sound of guitar and a voice, echoing through the microphone. Over the crowd and on the stage, a woman was leaning forward with the emotion of the song, and Sebastian watched as she sang the lyrics to Linkin Park's "Crawling." Her face beaded with sweat, her eyes squeezed shut, the tendons in her neck standing out while her hair, black streaked with blue hung over her face, covering her eyes.

"There she is, man," the guy said and looking at Sebastian watched him stare. "She's out of your league, trust me, man. She ain't for no one to take."

Sebastian looked at the man wearing the Nirvana tee shirt and asked, "What's the name of the band?"

The punk shook his head. "You got me," he said. "I listen to Nirvana. Kurt Cobain, till I die." He turned and walked back into the restaurant. Sebastian watched as the woman continued to sing, her voice as talented as that of Chester Bennington himself and it made Sebastian wonder how much she trained her vocal cords. As he watched, she tossed her head and then threw her body forward, belting out the last of the lyrics before the song ended and she stepped back, waving her hand in the air, speaking calmly which sounded like a shock as her screaming was so harsh it was as if she had been choking.

"Thank you, Duluth, Minnesota!"

People cheered, and others whooped. The crowd surged and then backed up. Sebastian pushed through and moved up to the wall, heading sideways towards the stage. As he watched, the singer continued to talk.

"Well, as you all know, I'm exhausted." She waited for the laughter to subside and then tucking hair out of her eyes, looked over to where she saw the man in the coat moving up, heading towards her. "Looks like we got someone who can't wait to say hi. I guess I should let him, right?"

The crowd booed and Sebastian felt people grabbing him, prodding him back towards the door. He shifted his weight and elbowed a man in the shoulder, driving him away, the woman behind him buckling, falling to the floor. The man behind her stumbled into the woman holding a beer that splashed across the other standing beside her. The two looked at one another and then all hell broke loose.

Sebastian watched the fight break out.

VII |

The woman covered in beer swung her full bottle of Michelob, smashing it over the second female's face, watching it shatter. There was a scream as glass sprayed over the floor and the stage. The people on stage stepped back as others in the audience staggered, some gaining momentum and moving towards the stage, others surging back, towards the exit. A few had already left, the door opening and then closing several times before the mass of bodies sealed it shut by the throng of moving legs and arms that cascaded; people striking, hitting, punching, biting, kicking, fighting. Among them, Sebastian was struggling to grab for his gun and as he reached the grip, he pulled it free, aiming the barrel in the air and firing off two rounds, felt the sudden movement surrounding him become stunned and still.

"All of you stop this madness now!" he called out over the still panicked haste. Looking at the many faces, some of them stained with beer and liquor, others by blood sweat and tears, he felt a longing for the factor of being in control and how he was still somehow struggling to maintain his position among the rest of them. Turning towards the stage, he looked at the gun and then staring at the safety, turned it on, slipping the weapon into the holster at his shoulder. Unclipping his badge, he flashed it to the crowd. "My name is Detective Lincoln Sebastian, I'm with the Duluth Police Department. I am here to speak with Skye Danes."

Feedback from a microphone followed by a groan from several people in the crowd and Sebastian swiveled on his feet. He saw the woman on stage looking at him, watching his expression of seriousness and serenity amongst the chaos.

"What do you want?" the singer asked.

Holding the picture still gripped in his hand, albeit now damaged and worn from the scuffle, Sebastian walked over and as he reached where the leader of the band stood, still holding the mic, waiting for his reply, he showed her the picture and watched her gaze at the image of family, her family, from years before.

"I've seen that before," Skye said. "Where did you get it?"

"It was in a file compiled from your father's murder case."

The singer looked at the detective, watching him stare back at her with sudden wonder as to what her reaction would be. Then, as the microphone dropped from her hand and her knees buckled, her body fell forward and towards the edge of the stage. He held out his arms, and caught her, just as everything in her world turned to black.

The crowd surrounding them stepped back as Sebastian carried the young woman to the door and then through the restaurant to a booth. He rested her in a seat and then called the waitress for a rag soaked in cool water. Placing it over her brow he waited patiently for the next several minutes until she had woken, and when she did, the realization that her father was dead hit her hard.

"I just can't believe it," Skye said, her eyes streaming tears that were blackened by the makeup she wore. "He's really gone . . . I . . . I have no other family. My grandparents are all dead. My parents had no other siblings."

Sebastian nodded, taking his time to allow the news to sink in and watching the singer of the cover band he had found was entitled Yris spelled with a "Y" instead of an "I" he felt a longing to help her somehow, but he couldn't think of any way to do that without misjudging how she felt about personal space. When she calmed down, he started by asking what she knew about a suitcase he had found with her initials in the basement of her father's home.

"I don't know," Skye said. "I didn't know he had one."

"Was there anyone who wanted to harm your father that you know of?"

"No, I mean, he had enemies, but they were all in his firm. They wished him failure on his cases but the most that happened was an email saying he should get the hell out of practice and find a better hobby. Something along those lines."

Sebastian nodded. He looked at the table and then smelled the aroma of food. Glancing at his watch he noticed it was already after two. He hadn't eaten lunch yet. "You hungry?" he asked.

Skye looked towards the other people who were devouring a late meal and nodded. "Starving," she said.

"Why don't we eat something, my treat, then we can move somewhere not so public and have more privacy."

The singer met his gaze and for the first time since the concert she smiled.

"That would be nice," she said.

Standing across the street in the downpour of rain, watching Skye Danes and the detective talk, the man in the black trench coat carrying the black umbrella could only imagine what was on his mind to be a truth that was to be foreseen in the future as a possibility, not a fact. He wanted it to happen, not to let it be a failure like his past. He knew it was only a matter of time before control took over and leniency of his judgement became a calling he could not suppress. He was feeling his rage build and it was intolerant. He wanted to grasp the man's heart, feel it pulsating in his hand, just before he squeezed, allowing it to burst, the contents of the organ flowing through his fingers in strands.

Hearing the click of heels to his right, he didn't turn his head, but felt a hand touch his shoulder and then lifting the umbrella if only a few inches, allowed the woman to come close by his side, under the shelter of the parasol.

"If it were so easy you could have done it already," she said.

The man bit his cheek, feigning the disinterest in the topic. He shook his head. It was never easy. It never had been. Years of planning and choices being made carefully just so he could make it this far in life, not that it would have been different if he had died. The fact that he was still here after the sudden tragedies of his past; all of it was a factor in his relationship against the law. The very thing that he had fought to defeat since being divided with the truth of his religion towards belief in belonging to something. What, he didn't know. Only now, after having been with this woman whom he trusted with his very life and loving her for whom she was to him; the fact that he would take a bullet for her was not a denial.

She was the only breathing being he cared for.

"What should we do next?" she asked him. "She's already found out about her father."

The man smiled, seeing the expression of both sadness and grief on Skye Danes' face through the window, the detective continuing to aide her through it all with his talent of relationships.

The thought disgusted him.

"We wait," he said.

"Until?"

The man turned, starting down the street.

"The investigation descends."

IX |

Sebastian arrived back at the office after six, sometime after dropping off the singer at the band's hotel, The Holiday Inn. Skye had calmed down enough to talk about her father's deeds in the firm and that his clients existed as others that wanted to cash out on better deals. He was a good attorney, other opinions had proved that theory, but someone had killed him, and it had been someone he knew. The door to the house hadn't been broken in, there had been no tampering with the lock, and there was no sign of a struggle. It appeared that Danes had allowed himself to be taken advantage of for the last time in his life, his dealings becoming his end as Skye had said; she felt he had only made choices that were careless and none of them had led him down the right path.

Sitting back down at his desk, he stared at the suitcase still on top and then wondering what to do next, looked at his phone, seeing no red light flashing to indicate he had any messages. Thinking of leaving for the day, he stood and tucking the case under the desk, walked out of his office, locking up behind him, and passing by a janitor who was vacuuming the floor, stepped on the cord that was connected to the wall, accidentally unplugging the outlet. The hum of the motor ceased.

"Hey, watch it, pal."

Sebastian apologized and plugged the cord back in, glancing over his shoulder at the man. He saw that he wore a cap and it featured the Chicago Cubs logo.

"Cubbies, huh?"

The janitor cut the power, looked up to meet his eyes. "What's that?"

"I said, the cubbies. You a fan?"

The man's eyes glanced up to the hat and he made a face, smiling sheepishly. "Oh, huh, yeah. I love the team. Great record. I think they won the last year, didn't they?"

Confused as to the man's reaction, Sebastian knitted his brow. "I don't know," he said, and waving his hand, walked to the doors. "Have a nice evening." He heard the vacuum pick up again, followed by the muttering of the janitor. Outside the rain had slowed to a drizzle, but there was still a chill in the air. He tightened his coat around himself and as he got to his car, climbed in behind the wheel, sliding the key in the lock. He felt his phone start to vibrate in his pocket and frowned, wondering who would be calling. Pulling it out he didn't recognize the number but answered, surprised to hear Skye's voice.

"Detective Sebastian," she said. "I wasn't sure you'd be awake. Or if you'd be busy for that matter."

Sebastian stared at traffic going by on Rice Lake Road. "I'm usually at work until later, but I've decided to go home," he said. "What's going on, is there something wrong?"

"Well nothing's wrong, it's just . . . I don't like to be alone."

"Aren't you with your band mates?"

"They left for the Cities."

"You mean—"

A sob was heard over the line. "We broke up. I couldn't keep it together after I told them my father was killed. They said it was just too much. I don't know what to do. They took the van and they left me here . . . I don't wanna be here by myself." She sniffed. "Will you come here and stay with me, or . . . could you pick me up?"

Sebastian closed his eyes. Personally, he would have thought that Skye Danes was someone of a stronger morale within a chain of friends. But it appeared that she was a broken shell from something far more fragile. He didn't think it was wise to connect with her and if it were so that she was able to feel anything except for heartfelt appreciation towards him and leave it at that he would be happy. Nothing personal.

Yet somehow, he was still wondering why he felt the need to be protective.

"Detective?" the voice sounded both panicked and frightened.

"Yeah," Sebastian said. "I'm on my way." He ended the call and set the phone in the cup holder, then driving from the lot headed through East Side into downtown to pick up Skye Danes.

X |

Sebastian pushed open the door to his house, switching on a lamp and revealing the living room in a yellow glow. He set his keys on the coffee table, turning around to see the singer following him in, her duffel bag over one shoulder, her face cleaned, hair still wet from having showered before he arrived to pick her up. She had cried on the way after leaving, to come here. He knew she was in pain, the band Yris having broken up, but still, it was something she would somehow try to cope with since her father's death had been a burden to bear and the group, she was in had not understood.

"There's fresh blankets laid out on the bed in the spare room down the hall," Sebastian said. "If you want, I can get you something, if there's anything that you need?"

Skye shook her head, swallowing, forcing her feelings back down. "I'll be fine," she said. "I'll sleep out here." Setting her bag on the floor next to the sofa she removed her shoes and laying down on the couch facing with her back to him she propped her bare feet up on the arm rest, curling her toes and crossing her arms against the cold, said, "Good night."

Sebastian nodded. "Night." He turned and walked towards the kitchen before hearing shuffling and then Skye's voice.

"You live alone?"

Glancing over his shoulder, Sebastian watched her stare at him in question. She was curious, as was everyone who had ever walked into his home. He sighed. It wasn't easy explaining things. The fact that he lived a life of solitude didn't bother him as much as it did everyone else.

"I do," he said, continuing to the fridge where he grabbed a bottle of Miller Lite and twisting off the cap took a long swallow, holding the chilled beverage in his hand. He stared at the floor, listening to silence.

"Was there anyone you ever loved?" he heard the singer moving, then stillness. "Like someone who you couldn't stay away from. Someone you wanted to be with the rest of your life?"

Sebastian took another drink of beer.

"No."

Silence followed by a softness in his heart he felt would be enough to kill him if there were a knife driven through like a stake in a vampire's chest. He closed his eyes and lowered his face, rubbing his eyes and squeezing them shut, dragged his fingers across his chin, feeling the growth of a month's stubble. He heard footsteps and opened his eyes only to see the singer standing in the kitchen before him, her gaze that of someone who was knowing what he felt as a lonesome longing for love. It wasn't between them; it was apart from each other. They had their own paths to take. Sebastian would work the case and find out that his own past was haunting him; she would figure out that her own life was taking a turn for the worst, but there was a better road ahead then the one that other people had taken to step away.

Staring at each other, the two people in the house waited for one or the other to speak. When nothing happened, Skye spoke up.

"So, did you want to talk about it?" she asked.

Sebastian stood, nursing his beer, didn't answer.

"You should get some sleep," he answered a moment later. "Take the spare bedroom, it's more comfortable. I'll see you in the morning." Leaving the beer on the counter, he walked down the hall. A second later a door was heard shutting, followed by the sound of a lock. A stillness filled the house. The singer stood alone in the kitchen, staring at the beer, watching the bubbles fizz. Then, turning and stalking back to the hall, she moved to the bedroom and walking in, got between the covers of the bed, and closing her eyes, allowed sleep to take her.

The offices of the Duluth Police Department remained dark, lit only by shadows cast in the glare of moonlight. Down the hall, through one of the open rooms, a single desk lamp glowed. The sound of banging could be heard followed by the harsh whispers of cursing. The form of a man appeared, wearing a cap with the logo for the Chicago Cubs. He grimaced as he stood from his crouch, heaving the object he was intending to take with him and looking towards the door, stared at the hall and the emptiness beyond; there was no one here, no witness who could thwart his possible plan.

Brushing sweat from his brow, he pulled the cap down over his face and then realizing his mistake, breathed a sigh of aggravation, setting the case next to the door as he closed it. Reaching into the bottom compartment of his cart, he pulled out a set of belongings and removing the cap and his uniform, he bundled them up, shoving them into the bag. Sealing it, he set it aside, in the corner of the room. Standing in his shoes and boxers, the man felt gooseflesh crawl across his skin. Shivering, he fought the urge to allow the fear to take him; it was only just that fate was to follow him, to make him fail. He had known this when he was given the instructions to raid the office and retrieve the case.

Simple, yet somehow, he wasn't so certain he had it down to a "T" as the man would have called it.

The man.

Standing in his undergarments, he felt the air grow colder, like ice. He took the bundle of belongings and pulling on a pair of pants, buttoned on a dark shirt, pulling on a coat and then raising the collar around his face, felt relief as he tightened the cloth around his midsection. He breathed a sigh of relief as he pulled on a hat, and then grabbing the pair of spectacles tucked into the front pocket of his shirt, he put them on, blinking as his eyes adjusted to the fake lenses.

Opening the door, he pushed the cart outside the office, leaving it in the hall. Returning, he took the case, and carrying it with him, closed the office behind him, turning the key and then pocketing the set, left the building, leaving behind nothing except for the mysterious fact that he and he alone had just broken in and out of the police department.

XI |

Sebastian woke to the sound of someone singing. He opened his eyes to see light filtering through the blinds and sitting up on the edge of the bed, listened intently to the sound of the melody. The song sounded familiar and he could almost make out the voice against the backdrop of female vocals.

Standing, he crossed to the hall and walking to the living room, found Skye laying on the couch, her feet propped up and her phone playing music. Her lips moved to form the lyrics to "I Am the Highway." He watched her eyes grow misty, but remain clear, as she stared at the ceiling, deeply filled with the emotion of Chris Cornell's voice.

As the song ended, she turned to him and squinting against the light of the sun that was cast from the glare on the living room windows, watched him smile.

"What?"

"Nothing," Sebastian said.

Skye furrowed her brow and then sighed. Tapping a few buttons on her screen she asked, "Did you like it?"

"Yes."

"Enough to say that I still have something?"

Seeing the way her eyes remained glassy, Sebastian could only imagine how she felt. Having been left behind, the group now in the Cities and her in Duluth, with a murderer on the lose having killed her father, Skye Danes was a victim. She was someone who would remain troubled, so long as there was a drag to make her feel she could no longer go on. The fact that he was there to help her no doubt made her feel comforted, but Sebastian had no intention of going beyond a professional relationship, let alone making himself connected in the sociality of the singer's byway.

"I think you do," he said, without lying. He was telling the truth. He believed she had something and that something was solid. She had a voice that was crafted as if by magic and it was useable to a certain extent, that if viable, could be spread far enough to be heard across a stadium with a microphone and heard by ears that were gone deaf to the most crucial of hearing loss.

Skye forced a smile, looking at her ankle and playing with the bracelet, glanced at the pictures on the wall. She saw only a man alone, either standing on Park Point, or drinking at a local bar. She wondered how he could work alone, and live alone, and stay sane. Let alone the fact it was a change in the matter of perspective that kept her from feeling an inch of sudden want to make him understand that she was the one who would care enough to change that.

Sebastian checked his watch and saw the time. "I have to get back to the office," he said. "Stay here and I'll be back. Don't answer the door, or the phone."

Skye watched him disappear into the bedroom, returning a moment later having showered and changed into a black dress shirt and tie with dress pants and wingtips. He pulled on a trench coat and clipped his badge to his belt, checking the safety on his .45 Beretta. He slipped the weapon into his shoulder holster and then turning to see Skye getting up waited while she walked over, surprising him with a sudden hug.

"Be careful," she said, resting her head on his chest. She closed her eyes, inhaling his scent. It was a warm comfort, sweet, yet soft. Sebastian gently patted her back and as she released him, he left, heading to his car. As he drove away, he realized how much she cared. Not since he had been young had he thought about being in love.

Now he realized how dangerous it could be.

XII |

Lieutenant Wayne Lovejoy squeezed the bridge of his nose between two fingers and closed his eyes before opening them to stare at the janitor's cart. He noticed the clothes that were shoved carelessly into the basket and the cleaning supplies that were not used, but empty, having been drained, only before the job was done. Looking at the door, he saw that it was locked and knew no one had entered since last night.

A brisk clicking of shoes on carpet and Lovejoy turned to face the man he was waiting for. Sebastian greeted him with a concerned stare.

"What is it?" he said.

"Well," Lovejoy said, "my secretary came in and said that she found this cart outside your office door . . . there are clothes in it. I was wondering myself why the janitor never came back, I mean why would he change clothes?"

Sebastian bit his cheek, glimpsing in his mind the last evening he had talked with the man in the Cubs baseball cap before leaving for the day.

Cubbies, huh?

What's that?

I said the Cubbies, you a fan.

Oh, huh, yeah. I love the team. Great record. I think they won the last year, didn't they?

"No," Sebastian whispered. He shook his head and grabbing for his keys, felt them jingle in his hand as he slipped one in the door, turning it. "No, no, no, no," he repeated, turning the knob and stepping inside. The air was clean as if nothing had been violated. Looking to his desk he walked over to the chair and pulling it back, crouched, staring under the mahogany to see the empty space.

"What is it, Lincoln?"

"*Shit!*" Sebastian smacked the flat of his hand on the top of his desk and standing, looked to his boss with a shake of his head. "The case is gone."

Lovejoy's look of grave disappointment turned grim. He glanced over his shoulder at the other men and women who were now standing at attention behind him, those who all knew that the impossible had happened.

The police department had been robbed.

"Get the footage," Lovejoy said, "see what you can find about this mysterious janitor." Turning to Sebastian he said, "I want you to go back to your house and watch that girl. Ask her some more questions. See what she might know. Otherwise I don't need you to come back, this is deep enough already."

"Are you certain this wasn't just a tactic to scare us out of our uniforms?" a female officer said. "I mean if he wants us to chase him then why not chase him?"

"Because, Mona," another male in plainclothes replied, "we have to find out who he is. What he wants. Why he's doing it."

"She's right though," Lovejoy said, and the woman smiled. "It's a chase he wants." Nodding to Sebastian he said, "Best of luck to you. I'll expect a call if you find anything. Let me know if you come on some sort of grounds as to making sense of this."

Sebastian watched the crowd of men and women disperse before returning to his desk and taking a seat behind it, waited until he had finally relaxed and felt comfortable to open the top drawer. He pulled out the file he was looking for that lay there and flipped it open, stopping short when he saw something that didn't belong.

A photograph, black and white, with block letters written in red ink on the face of the man dead for over three decades stared back at him, the features defined by lines that were of an age still young, that would remain young. As having been put that way by him; considering the eyes, Sebastian felt a chill. He read the words that covered the face:

YOU KNOW WHAT YOU DID

Breathing heavy, Sebastian slapped the folder closed and sat back in his chair, closing his eyes and hearing feet crossing the carpet, crossing his threshold, listened to the soft voice of a woman talking to him.

"Detective?" a pause. "Detective, are you all right?"

Sebastian opened his eyes. He blinked. He saw the beautiful lady who was young, who had a life ahead of her, staring back at him, smiling. She watched him gaze at her with sudden fear and pallor in his features.

YOU KNOW WHAT YOU DID.

"Yes, thank you, I'm . . . I'm fine." Sebastian cleared his throat. "Uh, could you ask Lieutenant Lovejoy if he could let me take a raincheck on that phone call. I need to talk to him right now."

The secretary, known only as Katie, nodded. Knitting her brow, she asked, "Are you sure you're fine?"

"Yes, I'm good."

"Okay." It sounded uncertain, but the woman left, returning a moment later with the boss in tow. Lovejoy stared at his detective's sudden nervous stature with both gruesomeness and heartfelt wonder. He waited until Sebastian collected himself to ask, "What do you have to show me?"

Sebastian slid the folder across to him, watching the lieutenant cautiously look at the file. "Open it," he said, and Lovejoy peeled back the cover, eying the black and white photograph of the image that portrayed a man who had been one of their own, but who had been lying in the grave for the past thirty-three years.

"Well," he said after a moment that felt too long to the detective.

"What do you think?" Sebastian asked. "Is it who I think it is?"

Lovejoy pursed his lips, closing the file after another beat. "Yes. It is." He looked at his watch. Turning to Katie he spoke to her in a whisper and as she left, he looked to Sebastian. "I want you to tread carefully. If this is what I am of the mind to believe, then you, and Skye, are in grave danger."

"Why is Skye in any danger? I was the one who.?"

"Skye is a loose end. She'll no doubt react upon the fact that when she finds out how and why you are the one to begin this in the first place, she'd want to stay away. I want you to make sure she stays put."

"What about Sean's wife?"

"I'll handle her. Meanwhile, you take the evening and relax. I don't need this office more riled up than it already is. You know when I say that this is a big step; the past is catching up. And when the fire is hot, it is going to burn each and everyone one of us in this department, starting with you and me. So, I want you out. I want you off this case. Do I make myself perfectly clear?"

"Sir . . ."

"I am not going to say this again. Do I or do I not make myself serenely positive?"

Sebastian swallowed his pride. He gave up on fighting the man he knew would only win trying to help. Standing from his desk without another word he left, and feeling a pat on his back, was out the door to his car, knowing that behind him, Lovejoy was watching him every step of the way, having his back like he'd always had, for the past thirty-three years of his life.

XIII |

His wingtips clicked on the catwalk as he stood a story above the work floor. He smelled the odor of wooden shavings and felt the heat surrounding him amongst the lights. He tasted bitterness of the mint gum on his tongue and swallowed dryly, wishing he had water.

Seth Kent, newly appointed assistant manager of Verso Company continued through the second-floor area of the building, making sure everything was as it should be. Workers were either finishing their days or returning for the night shift. He smelled the aroma of his cologne and felt somehow enticed by the odor of Bod spray which he put on just about every morning. He hated the way it tasted if he had his mouth open and it always seemed to be one of those things that failed to impress his girlfriend. She hated the aroma and wanted him to "throw the damn thing out" as it were.

Stepping into the air-conditioned offices he walked by a printer that was finished making a page and pulling it out, ran his finger down the numbers before finding the sentence he was searching for. Nodding to himself he hummed a tune and crossed to his desk, a glass walled cubicle with a deadbolt door. He took a seat and picking up a pen tapped a few keys on his computer, still humming the tune. A moment later he heard a knock on his door, interrupting his work.

"Yes, come in?"

Ryan Rayburn entered, carrying a Frappuccino. He set it on the desk before his new assistant manager and watched the man happily take several long pulls on the straw.

"Thank you." Kent tasted the salted caramel. It was good.

"Yes, it seems that our sales have gone up," Rayburn said with a smile. "Thanks to you. Your ethics in this line of work is so well put that I should soon be seeing you having my job."

Kent chuckled. "Oh, no, no, I couldn't," he said. "I would find that too offensive as to . . . why are you staring at me like that?"

Rayburn gazed at the man openly and as he continued to smile, his face broadened into an ivory grin.

"You are really something, you know that?" Rayburn's awkward stare turned into a gaze. "It just makes me feel awful sometimes to see other people not so better off. I think that I should be giving them a raise." He paused, shaking his head and then added, "Just remember to be careful. Things can change for the worse. You never know what can happen. Even work can become dangerous."

Kent frowned. "How so?"

"Well, take the steamrollers for instance. We had a guy who fell in front of his own steamroller. It wasn't a pretty sight. This world ain't like *Who Framed Roger Rabbit* and you ain't gonna blow yourself back up with no tank."

Kent felt queasiness as the salted caramel touched his gut. "What happened to the worker?'

"Unfortunately, with no one to man it, the guy was flattened like a pancake. So, you should just be careful." He tapped his hand on the door panel and smiled. "Enjoy your coffee, assistant manager. I'll be coming to check on you again sometime."

"Yeah, see you then." Kent waited for his door to close and the shadow of his boss to fade before he took another drink of the coffee. Then, focusing on the papers in front of him to the best of his mind's extent, he found that thoughts of death were no longer on his conscience but fading and he no longer felt fear.

It all faded like the fog that covered his mind as if in a fairy tale hollow.

Sebastian sat in his recliner, staring at the far wall and listening to the sound of the rain hitting the roof, the pounding of water as it ran through the gutter, rushing through metal in a torrent before draining to the ground. Thunder rolled in the distance, echoing the passing storm as it continued over Duluth. He saw lightning flash and felt that summer was not only going to be just alike, but the same as this. The weather was unintelligible, if anything it mattered to the tourists for warmth in the forecast. He felt he had no say in that. Now with him off the case, he would stray from being public if he wanted to keep from being seen by the killer. Duluth was such a small city, and so closed in, that you could hide, but depending on where you were from and how well you knew the area you could find out where people were and when. What time of day it was and why they were there? Sebastian's instinct had taught him over years of being a cop and after becoming detective, he had crafted it, growing more aware over coming years.

Watching the grandfather clock, he took a sip of the screwdriver he had made and grimaced at the flavor. It was already after seven and he was still without dinner. He didn't care to eat. He didn't care to sleep. He didn't want much of anything except to be on the case, let alone to protect the singer who was sleeping in the room down the hall. She had gone to bed early tonight, sometime after he had arrived to tell her the news that he had been removed from the investigation. Although unhappy, she didn't seem too upset, aside from the fact that she knew the reason behind his mood and making an alcoholic drink as soon as he walked through the door.

Shaking her head, she had gone to the bedroom and closed the door. After several minutes he went to check and found her asleep, between the covers, her back turned to him as she rested.

Sebastian eyed the living room window, watching traffic go by on the street outside, and wondered how he was supposed to stand much longer with the ghost of his past come to haunt him. Still, as he thought about it, the message scrawled in red ink came back to him:

YOU KNOW WHAT YOU DID

Shaking his head in disbelief of his sudden misunderstood fear, Sebastian drained the rest of the screwdriver, which was still half, and pulling his lips back against his teeth, felt the burn of alcohol warm his insides as he stood, turning. He stopped when he saw who stood in the hallway, watching him.

"Skye," he said, "I thought you were asleep?"

Skye blinked, yawning as she stepped towards him, then eying his expression, said, "I had a nightmare." As her hands dropped to her sides, she stared at him, tired and with a question on her mind. Her lips moved, her tongue thick: "Could I sleep with you, tonight?"

Sebastian furrowed his brow and stammered. "What?" seeing the young woman gaze at him openly now, her eyes growing suddenly wet he feared the worst as she spoke with a broken voice.

"Please," Skye said, "I don't want to be alone right now. I'm scared." She added, "I promise it's only for tonight. I just don't want to be by myself."

Feeling the oddity, but still understanding, Sebastian sighed as he watched Skye wipe away the tears that were forming on her cheeks. "Fine," he said. "But only for tonight."

"Thank you." Skye turned and walked down the hall, stopping when she noticed he was still behind. "Are you coming?"

Sebastian set the empty crystal on the coffee table and followed her to his bed. Skye pulled aside the sheets, climbing between them and then curling up, patted the spot beside her as she rested her head on the second pillow. As Sebastian climbed into bed, on top of the sheets, the singer wrapped herself next to him, resting her hand on his chest as she nuzzled her head in the crook of his shoulder. She breathed him in and smiled.

"You smell good," she whispered. "Kind of like Hugo Boss."

Sebastian said, "I don't wear cologne."

A silence passed before Skye murmured, "Your natural smell." He felt her move and then her breath was on his neck and she said, "I wish you'd feel more comfortable towards women."

He frowned. "I'm not gay."

"I never said that."

Sebastian sighed. "I just prefer the single life. It's easier for me."

Skye snorted. "Better you mean?" he heard the smile in her voice. "A bachelor's life, Detective. You're single-minded. It's funny."

"What's funny about it? I don't want to challenge the fact that if I do find someone, I care about that they'll be hurt."

A pause. "You mean someone like me?"

Sebastian found himself stuck as he thought for a moment. The bed shifted and he felt Skye moving before she was above him, looking down. Her hair covered her eyes, shielding her gaze as she watched him. He saw she was curious for his answer. When he didn't tell her right away, she spoke.

"You care about me?" she said. Her eyes knitted and then her hand touched his face and she cupped his cheek, cradling his chin, almost tenderly. Leaning forward their lips brushed one another before she kissed him and Sebastian tasted her, felt her tongue parting his, their organs connecting. He murmured a question and she silenced him with a finger to his lips as she sat up, removing her shirt. She wasn't wearing a bra and as the lightning flashed, he saw her bare skin, a winged tattoo shading the right side of her body, from below her breast to her navel, circling like a tail. He watched the diamond piercing in her navel reflect the next flash of lightning before she took his hand and pressing it to her left breast, whispered, "If you care, then show me."

Looking in her eyes, Sebastian couldn't deny his fortune of love for who this woman was. He knew now that despite having been unable to, despite having been able to care for anyone besides his own family, he had left nothing but emptiness in his heart and forsaking each person who had tried to be there for him, as a friend, as a companion, he had ignored that right given to him countless times.

As their bodies connected Sebastian forgot all about the investigation and the message from his past that come to haunt him.

| Part Two |

| Three Months Later |

XIV |

The grass was covered with an evening dew. As Chastity Connors jogged the muddied path into the Lester River trail, her eyes stared ahead, watching the leaves and the winding route that wove through the wood. She smelled the aroma of the late August afternoon and could tell by the shade of gray from above that it was going to rain sometime soon. She would have to find a faster route this time, be certain not to tread too slow and if it did start to pour, make it to the gazebo for shelter, where no more than a year before, Justin, her boyfriend of seven years, had proposed to her, under the moonlight. She had said "yes" and was blessed. Justin had proved that he loved her, that he wanted to share his life with her. It was enough that even her parents had said they wanted her to tell him he had their blessing.

As she followed the path through the wood, passing the first and second bridges before reaching the third, she felt the breeze passing through strands of her dark auburn hair and blinked away the stinging sweat that filled her eyes, brushed a sleeve across her face slowing as she took a moment to catch her breath and looked left to stare through the gaps of the pine trees. She saw the area of rocks and the face of the hillside that sloped down towards a pool of water formed by the falls flowing under the nearby swinging bridge. Squinting, her eyes refocused and she noticed what appeared to be a body resting against the rocks themselves, a person she believed was either asleep, or worse, injured.

"Hey!" Chastity called. "Are you all right?"

There was no answer from the human who rested at the foot of the falls. Chastity checked the time on her watch and realized it was getting late. In a few more hours it would be dark. Mosquitos hummed and buzzed, and she swatted a few as they tried to bite her neck and face. Turning, she took off at a jog, rounding to the bridge as she stopped to look more closely at the person who seated against the hill. Now, as she neared, she noticed something else. Resting at their side, a young child was cuddled. This worried the hiker, and Chastity panicked, wasting no time in moving to where the trees met the rocks and the hill sloped towards the edge of the water. She looked over again, still unable to tell who the person was, woman or man. As she gripped the rock wall, she found it hard to hold, the slick moss and moisture having gathered over time and with the day as muggy as it seemed, she carefully maneuvered her way down, slipping only once but catching herself as she hugged the hill, feeling her body covered by the mud that caked the sheet of stone and marble.

Once her feet touch the surface below, Chastity glanced up at how high the climb would be and cursed her luck before turning to face the body. As she caught a glimpse of the woman, she realized how odd it had seemed, but now up close, it seemed even more frightening.

The young female was dressed in a red satin outfit, with bally slip-ons, her skin a milky pallor and her face painted. There were lines where her jaw would shift to make it appear as if the bones unhinged. Her eyes were open, and makeup had been applied to show blush on her cheeks. Her gaze strayed forward and even in death, her stare was glassy, as if her eyes were fake.

Chastity swallowed dryly, searching for the child and finding what she had thought was a baby seated beside the woman, its focus in the same direction, she parted her lips, wetting them with her tongue before stepping back, and then again, before stopping short as her heel rested on nothing but air. She tumbled back, feeling the shock of cold, fish-tasting water before she kicked to the surface and grabbing the ledge stared at the doll. Its smile was wicked, the leering ivory of a face that was freckled with sharp blue eyes and blonde hair. His suit was charcoal and his shirt starched white, the tie a blood red. Chastity heard a noise, like the crunch of a footstep, and listened to the air, hearing laughter, like the giggle of a child. Then, as she saw the figure standing high on the ridge of the hill, near the gazebo, knew there was nothing she could do to keep the sound from escaping her.

The man's face was covered by a baby doll's, cut and shaped to his, a hood over his head. The rest of his body was cloaked in black, his large build making up for the tinny voice that came from his mouth.

As Chastity screamed, she thought of Justin and her body felt cold as she saw the red dot blinding her before the world went dark. There was nothing to stop the voice that spoke the words, hauntingly chill. She never forgot them, even as her body was thrown into the water from the force.

"Why are you so scared?" the child's voice said. "I just want to play a game."

XV |

The door opened and Detective Lincoln Sebastian strode in, walking the hallway carpet with his hands shoved in his pockets as he kept his eyes forward, focused on the path ahead. As he reached the door he was looking for, he turned to it, sliding his key into the lock and turning, twisted the knob, pushing. The wooden entryway creaked open on unoiled hinges and he smelled the musty aroma of old carpet and mahogany along with filed papers and folders. He inhaled it with a welcoming feeling that it was all his and his to own before stepping across the threshold and taking his seat at the desk, sitting back in the swivel chair and adjusting the backrest to his liking folded his arms, gazing at the dusty mahogany work space which was as he had left it except for one thing.

The file folder involving the case from May was gone.

Shaking his head and rubbing his temples as if to ease the pressure on his mind, Sebastian knew it wasn't enough to make him forget the message that had been printed on the image for him to read. It was a warning no doubt, something to tell him he was getting to close. The fact that his past had caught him unaware, to catch up with him after three decades, haunted him to the core. He wanted nothing more than to let it be and pass on to the next investigation.

It wasn't to be.

Shortly after retiring to the solitude and finding himself falling for the singer who was now with him in his bed, he had felt nothing but hardship and the realization that if he ever let his guard down, he would fail to keep Skye safe. He found his feelings for her growing and wondered how far he would go to the extent of making it possible for the killer to get close. As far as he knew the identity was still unknown, but he would know soon.

A knock sounded on the door and Lieutenant Lovejoy stood in the doorway, waving a new folder in his hand. "Got a fresh one for you," he said. "Turns out a jogger went missing in Lester Park. Earlier yesterday afternoon a family said they heard a noise, sounded like a gunshot." He shook his head and waved his arm in an arc as if to indicate a motion of grandeur. Something larger than the fact that involved the notion of truth about the case. "I want you to handle this yourself. I have someone who is willing to work with you on the case. She's no rookie. Been a detective on the force for only a few years but like her father has the hardened soul of a policemen."

Sebastian nodded, coughing into his hand. "Don't doubt it," he said. "So, you want me to partner up? What's this girl's name?" he took the folder from his boss, opening it to read the contents.

"Mallory Grey," Lovejoy said.

"Sounds seasonal."

"Well, I wouldn't tell her that."

Sebastian closed the file, standing from his desk and grabbing his keys exited his office. Looking over his shoulder he said, "Don't worry, I won't get too close to that aspect of conversation."

"Be certain you don't," Lovejoy said. He watched his detective depart and then turned back, walking to his office, standing in the doorway as he saw the person seated behind his desk, going through the file that was sitting on top of the oak. "Who the hell are you?"

The man did not glance up. He did not stand up. Instead, he raised a hand, and in it, he held something silver. It was a moment before Lovejoy recognized the weapon aimed at his chest, with the suppressor screwed to the barrel. By then it was too late for him to react.

Three shots rang out in the department, all three hitting home. The lieutenant of the Duluth Detective Bureau dropped to the floor of his office, his hand still resting on his gun as if by a slim chance he had any hope of gaining control of the situation. As the man behind the desk stood, sliding the weapon into the folds of his coat, he tucked the folder under his arm, crossing the room and stepping over the body of the lieutenant, passed by the first plainclothes woman to enter the head office. She was in shock at first, stunned to see what had happened so swiftly. When she turned to call out, hand reaching for her gun, the figure spun, hand withdrawn, aimed dead center and firing. The third eye sprouted between the woman's gaze and she fell backward over Lovejoy.

Other officers drew their weapons, and the man with the file folder turned to face them.

"On your knees!" a detective yelled. "Drop the gun, *now!*"

The figure slowed, gazing into the eyes of the many who were trained on him. As he watched the turmoil surrounding him, caused by his hand, he smiled, flashing a grin to the people in the hallway. The secretary screamed as she watched him get on his knees, still holding the gun but no longer aimed at the targets in mind. Pressing the heated barrel to his temple, the man eased his finger on the trigger and pulled.

As brains and viscera exploded in the air like confetti and blood sprayed the wall and carpeting, the detectives and officers who had watched everything and survived the turmoil could only imagine what would happen now that the lieutenant was shot. The reality was that as soon as the order was given and the file that was to be stolen was returned, the case involving a three-decade old murder of an officer of the law would be cracked wide open.

Detective Lincoln Sebastian would be investigating his worst nightmare.

XVI |

By the time he arrived at the park and saw the flashing strobe lights and lined up cars he knew it wasn't a good sign. Walking the muddied path and ducking the line of yellow tape that blocked the swinging bridge, Sebastian flashed his ID to the officers standing duty there before heading to the area of trees that lined a second path winding back toward the road and parking lot. He saw a gazebo to his right and a water fall with a pool centered. Standing under the protective roof of the gazebo, a burgundy haired young woman wearing a black turtleneck with coat and slacks had her arms folded and was surveying the scene. She saw him and strode over, extending a leather gloved hand.

"Detective Lincoln Sebastian?"

"Lincoln," he said. "You must be Mallory?"

She nodded. Turning to stare over the railing and at the edge of the rocks below she pointed a finger at the body resting at the bottom of the hill. "Looks like we found a Jane Doe," she said.

"We have any information?"

"Looks like a hiker, single bullet wound to the head. Not a close range. Positioned there." She indicated the rocks. "Her face is painted like a doll's."

Sebastian watched the technicians who were at the foot of the hillside, working to extricate the body. As one of them sorted the pockets, checking for evidence, the person discovered something, holding it out to show the two detectives standing on the bridge. He called out, "We got something!"

"Bring it up," Sebastian said, "I'm not going down there."

Heaving a sigh, the tech clambered up the hill and as he reached the top, staggered, brushing off his pants before meeting them at the gazebo, handing over the piece of paper. Mallory took it with a gloved hand, staring at the written message.

It read:

Dearest Detective,

You have come this far to find out who I am, if you want to know who I can be you will never know. The fact that there is something more to learn than you are far from it. I am sorry to say the hiker only failed to complete the task I set out to make. I wanted to play a game. I am only that of the mind which a child has when he grows. I make things easy for those who chose the right path. I design the matters in which growth can be compensated.

I am the black in which you cannot see. I am the panic from which you cannot breathe.

I am the Mannequin.

"It makes no sense," Mallory said.

"It's not supposed to," Sebastian said. "He's acting like a child. He wants to play a game." Turning back to walk the way he had come he called over his shoulder, "Let's go."

Mallory handed the note back to the tech and removing her glove, shoved it in her pocket. "Where are we going?"

"Back to the office," he said. "I have a feeling we can find out more if we dig in the past. This must be connected in some way to the reality from which I ran. Thirty-three years from now I'll be too old to fight this, I don't want to be dead in my grave and for him to win."

"You mean your past?"

Sebastian stopped. He turned to face the detective and watched her gaze at him knowingly. Her ocean blue eyes hardened to match his.

"I know about your past, Lincoln," Mallory said. "I studied your case. You're not the only one who has enemies. I tried to track down the person responsible for the killing of Sean Miller and yet there was no one. Now I need you to tell me you're not out for yourself on this one."

"Why would you care?"

"Because I have a partner."

Sebastian stared. He watched her remain unblinking. When she didn't move, he sighed. Turning he stalked in the direction of his car.

"Is that a yes?" Mallory called.

"If you can learn to trust what your gut says," Sebastian said, over his shoulder.

"And what's that?"

Sebastian kept walking. He didn't look back as he replied, "I never keep my promises."

XVII |

Both detectives strode through the doors of the department to find the carnage and mayhem having unfolded before they arrived. As they watched the stretcher that held the fitted sheet over the first body being moved across the carpeted floor, Sebastian turned his eyes to the wall near the door surrounding Lovejoy's office. He saw the blood splatter and pink matter of brain tissue. Stepping in the direction of the door he was halted by a hand on his shoulder, firmly keeping him from going any further. He looked over his shoulder, glancing at the plainclothes man who was there, stronger than he, but not as clear in mind. The cop released his grip and Sebastian walked the length of the hall past the mess of matter that had been made by the crime to the open door which yawned, welcoming anyone who entered, but with great consequence. He noticed as he looked in, the dark mass of spread crimson on the carpet, black against the already opaque carpet. He smelled the odor of it as it assailed his nostrils, feeling the familiarity of the essence and keeping to the corner near the wall, he gazed at the desk, eying the pages and papers that were misplaced. Moving toward the desk he heard a creak of the floor behind him. Reaching for his weapon he spun and with his hand on the grip hesitated, staring into the eyes of his new partner as she looked back at him gravely.

"He's at the ICU," Mallory said, "being treated for three bullet wounds to the chest. They say it's possible he could make it, but still he's lost a lot of blood and—"

"He'll make it." Sebastian swallowed hard. He let his hand drop from his gun and turned back to the desk, moving to investigate the clutter. As he stared at the folder which had been opened, he saw the image of the photograph which had been left on the oak to be seen. The same one from three months before when he had first discovered the message printed in red ink letters on a face that haunted him.

"They haven't identified the killer," Mallory said. "They say he was in here looking through the file from three decades ago. What would someone want with that?"

He shook his head. He felt sweat beading on his lip and wiped a sleeve across his mouth. Biting his tongue to keep from cursing, he blinked, feeling his eyes burn from the perspiration and then, watching the picture remain unmoving, still stuck in time, felt relief.

"I need to go check on Skye." Turning to Mallory he said, "You keep up to speed on the identity of the killer and see what you can find out about him."

"What about Lieutenant Lovejoy?"

Sebastian was already walking out of the office. He slowed, stopping as he reached the second body being hauled out on a stretcher. A woman, young, in her late twenties. He knew her. She had a younger sister and a boyfriend as well a family that had loved her. Now they had lost a sister, a daughter, a friend. Shaking his head, he looked at his partner and nodded.

"He'll be okay," he said. Turning he started back outside, and left Mallory at the department wondering if he still believed his own lie.

He wondered if it would follow him to his grave.

Seth Kent rocked back in his chair, gripping his face and moaning. He tasted blood, feeling with his tongue where the gap was in his teeth and knowing as he opened his eyes against the sting of crimson that it wasn't over yet. It would never be over. Not until the answer was given correctly.

Around him, the office was trashed. The waste baskets were emptied, guts on the floor, there were papers and files on the carpet as well as filing cabinets in the way of him trying to escape. He only knew as he recognized the scent of gunpowder that he could see the carnage was made by two people. The man had not come alone. A woman was with him; somewhere in the plant he heard screams, followed by the distant sound of an engine and something else, something he discerned to be realistically grotesque but couldn't place. A nightmare, only it was factual and could happen to him or anyone.

The man with the gun came forward again, and pointing the barrel in his face, curled his teeth back in a snarl. Kent saw the age in his face, but they weren't lines. It was in his hair. The roots had grown from black to white. He wore a pressed black suit and trench coat that hung around his legs and it dominated his slender yet muscular form. The menace was intruding as well as cross—he would not be crossed by anyone.

"Tell me what you know," the voice spoke harshly, hissing. "I want to know what you have on file about Sean Miller. What were his associate's planning to do with Kyle Danes stocks and bonds? Verso keeps a system, I know this. I had someone who used to work here long before you were even born. Now don't fuck with me. Tell me the *truth*." Pressing the barrel into the man's temple he eased his finger on the trigger. "What was Sean Miller hiding in the file?"

Kent stammered, "What—What file?"

The gun hand came up, then arced, down, harshly across the back. Kent groaned as his body fell over the desk, spreading mucus, blood, snot, all in a smear over the pages that had been scattered on the workstation. In the distance of the factory he heard a high-pitched scream, followed by choking. Then, suddenly it stopped. Sobbing, he sat up, rigid, forcing the pain away with all his muster and as he held up his hands to show he had nothing, said, "I don't know what he had on file. I don't know what he was protecting. I just know that he worked here. I started here after him. I was given his job. They don't tell me anything about past workers. The only person who could have told you something was Mr. Rayburn; I only do the filing. I just handle the papers. If something was lost on file—"

"It had better be found," the man said and held the gun trained on the man's forehead. He watched the eyes cross, grown bloodshot from beating. "Now I'm gonna count down from ten. When I make it to five, you had better have answer for me, buddy, or you will be seeing the next bullet out of this gun." Inclining his head, he touched his finger to the trigger. "Ten."

"Wait—!"

A gunshot echoed through the office. Splattered blood hit the back wall of the cubicle and covered the desk. Seth Kent slumped in his chair; a bullet hole centered in his forehead. The gun barrel that the man held was not smoking. Behind him, the click of heels could be heard clacking as the woman strode in and he caught a whiff of her perfume, inhaling it as he saw her blowing on her gun, sliding it back into her holster. Smiling she watched his expression sour.

"I told you I could handle it," he said sternly.

"Put it away," she said and leaned against the desk, watching her partner shove his weapon into the folds of his coat. "I got what we needed from his boss." She wrinkled his nose. "Sorry to say his life didn't end as quick and painlessly as this guy."

"So? What do we have?"

"Sean Miller took the secret with him to his grave. What we have is the case."

The man slammed his fists down on the desk and then standing and in a rage, charged through the office and onto the work floor, tearing apart a walled cubicle.

"Quiet down," she said after a moment or two of his upset, "we don't need any more problems between letting things get as far as they've gone and you losing your cool. Besides, there's someone new in the game. He calls himself "The Mannequin" makes his victims look like dolls."

The killer spun to face the woman, staring at her coldly. "What does this have to do with what we need on Skye Danes?"

"Danes is a project in the making. Leave it be for now. Like you said. The case is descending. The lieutenant lives. As soon as we find out how to open the case and we get that file we'll have the detective in our hands and be able to destroy him," the woman walked over and as she reached him, she touched his face gingerly, cupping his cheek. Her lips moved against his as they kissed, tenderly. When they parted their eyes met and he smiled.

She was right.

The pair left the factory, leaving the bodies of the workers behind and the man in the office to be found after an anonymous call was made to the police by someone paid to break the scene. Hours later, the two had moved on to their next victim: Skye Danes.

XVIII |

Thunder rolled in the sky and Skye sat up in bed, soundlessly woken from her dream. A peaceful dream that was carelessly ceased by the imaginary hand of a sudden nightmare that haunted her. The feeling of being alone.

Clutching the bedclothes to her body, even though she wore pants and a shirt, she shivered, and then dragging them with her as she stood, she crossed the bedroom to the door and looking down the hallway saw the shaft of lightning as it flickered from the bedroom window. Glimpsing the shadows cast on the floor from the manufactured structures that surrounded her in the emptiness of quiet, the singer swallowed dryly, feeling thirst as she stepped, bare foot onto the wooden boards that served as a path and rubbing her eyes, yawned, blinking tiredly as she headed into the living room and glancing through the open blinds saw that the black Audi was gone, leaving the driveway empty. Feeling her flesh crawl at the intensity of knowing she was by herself and had been for an unknown time, Skye bit her bottom lip, heading into the kitchen. She opened the fridge and grabbed a bottle of beer and removing the top took a long swallow before grimacing at the flavor. She stared at the label and shook her head, shrugging and taking another drink before turning to see the time on the stove. It was already after five and she felt hunger striking her in the gut with an iron hand. She was sure she could find something to eat.

A moment passed as she stood. Silence. She could almost hear the noise of the wind whistling as it whipped rain restlessly against the panes. She smelled the aroma of something strong, like cologne that Sebastian had used and as she waited for him, she knew it wasn't a thought that had triggered her feelings, but her need. She had wanted him as he'd wanted her. She was certain there was a connection. If anything changed, she would know.

If separation were the key, to become apart from Yris, it was only that she could exist as one and only, a human by her lonesome, just with a man who she could feel that she loved. The sex between them had been vigorous, the moments of clinical between them like explosions in the night. Fireworks of a love affair that had bonded them together. But in his eyes, she saw something, a piece of life that had been drained long ago. She still didn't know if she could trust him as much as he trusted her. Or if he didn't trust her should she still allow him to keep her in his home, away from what he called danger?

A shifting of the light and beams crossed the floor, traveling the walls and then, a squeal of wet brakes. Skye looked out the window to see the shadow of a man walking the path to the door and as he entered the house, she saw him stand in the doorway, drenched, and soaked by the rain. He removed his coat and tossed it on the couch, sitting down and kicking off his shoes. Rubbing his eyes, the person who owned the house covered his face and sat forward, flexing his arms to tension that had built up from the day.

Walking over to him, Skye sat down and lifting the bedsheets, put them over him as well as held them together over herself. She watched him glance at her, with tired eyes and his focus was on the face she gave him.

"What?" he said.

"What happened, today?' she asked.

Sebastian sighed, shaking his head. His hair was wet, and it dripped as if in a movie framed dramatically by the eyes that watched him on the screen. Skye reached up to touch his cheek, tenderly, lovingly and saw his skin shift, transforming into a grimace.

After a moment of quiet between them, Skye took his head and as he leaned into her embrace, his head resting against her chest, she kissed his forehead and she felt him grow comforted, felt him give into her touch. She rubbed his back, and knew it was only her that could feel the pain, knew it was only she who could understand the reform of their new relationship which was now folded and since Skye knew how Sebastian was uncertain, how he could be undone and she could just as well be over with how they were for each other, she wanted nothing more than to have it, one last time. To know what it was like to love again.

Standing, Skye took Sebastian's hand and leading him to the bedroom, closed the door behind them, their passion lighting up the night once again, and for one more time she felt that something had been done to keep them together.

They were in love.

That was how she felt.

XIX |

The room smelled of disinfectant, an odorless taste on his tongue as he stood amongst the dead themselves, wallowing in the luxury of what would be his resting place soon enough, was he not careful with his choices.

Staring at the sheet which covered the deceased form of the man who had laid an attack on the police department before putting a bullet in his own head, Detective Lincoln Sebastian took a deep breath and repositioning the mask on his face grimaced behind it, wincing at the pain in his left shoulder and the stiffness it brought. He'd been up for nearly six hours, ever since the storm of the night had brought him out of his mares and aroused him from the dream in which he was fighting a ghost—and losing. Skye was naked against him, her form fitted in his arms and he watched her rest, until dawn broke through the blinds in a blinding light. Her eyes had opened, and she looked at him, smiling slightly, brushing her hand over his face and running her fingers through his hair.

"Hey," she said.

"Hey," he said.

"You sleep well?"

"Mm."

Staring up at him then, she had watched his face remain emotionless, and unreadable. It was something inside it that bothered her.

"What's wrong?"

Sebastian sighed. "There's nothing wrong."

"Something's not right. It's bothering you."

He shook his head. Meeting her eyes, he watched them twinkle in the light from the curtains and then after the passing of a heartbeat he bit his tongue in thought. She was right. He was fighting the feeling that something was going to happen to one of them or both. He didn't want this to continue and with the investigation happening on its own, he was struggling to find out who was responsible.

Now, standing in the morgue, waiting for the sheet to be pulled, to reveal the cold corpse on the metal bed, the body of a shell of a man who had once been living and had been a criminal in another life, Sebastian felt the draft of a chill air that threatened to make him shiver. He fought the feeling and closed his eyes, swallowing hard. Feeling a hand on his arm he opened them and saw his partner, Mallory, gazing at him knowingly.

"You okay?" she asked.

He forced back on the bit in his head and the memories of past instances that could happen. Nodding he looked to the coroner. "Show me," he said.

Arthur Dennison, the M.E., eased the sheet down over the chest and revealed the head and shoulders, bare from the neck down. The skin had grown a shade of snowy white and the hair was a darker shade of black, mixed with a rusty brown in the spot where the bullet had been fired to enter the brain. Mallory breathed a groan of disgust, covering her mouth as she stepped back a bit. Dennison didn't waste his time, using his gloved hands to gently lift the head and pointing at the scalp and clotted tissue said, "This is where the bullet exited the brain. The matter as I was told is that the rest of the blood and viscera was on the walls of the department itself if I am to be corrected."

"No, you're right," Sebastian said, wincing as he imagined a heated projectile passing through someone's temple and exiting the back of their head. He remembered the crime scene and couldn't escape the fact that it had happened only hours ago. Leaning forward, he stared at the corpse's features, asking, "Did we find out who this guy is?"

The M.E. removed his mask, leaving it against his chest. He pursed his lips grimly and met the other man's eyes. "I'm sorry to say, Lincoln, that this one is also close to home."

Sebastian frowned. "What do you mean?"

Dennison held up a finger and crossed over to a desk cabinet where he pulled open a drawer and grabbing something within, came back to the table and handed the file over to Sebastian. The detective took it, removing his mask and staring at the title on the folder blinked. He found the name to be confusing but at the same time it haunted him.

MORIARTY.

"I figured since it had been years since you had found out about the family." Dennison pointed to what Sebastian held in his hand. "Everything you need will be in there." He paused, blanching and then shook his head, digging into his pocket. "Oh, and this is important as well. It was in his pocket." He handed the flash drive over and as Sebastian took it, he saw the look on his face grow sour.

"Believe me, Detective," the M.E. said, "you have no idea what you're getting yourself into."

XX |

The Mannequin sat alone, unnoticed at the café table, staring at his next victim. Her hair was golden, and she was beautiful, with ocean colored eyes, blue like the sky and silvery like the moon. Her face was oval, and her lips were blush, pink and fleshy. Smooth he was certain, almost silky to touch. Closing his eyes, he imagined the texture of paint and makeup applied, the color of shade to make her as he wanted, to show her as he would to the detective, to reveal her to the public of scrutinizers what it was like to become "made" by the hand of a person. The be given posture and rigid form, to be known as a true "doll" or "image" instead of being what you are to those who wanted you to be their friend.

None of what he held in his mind was right or had been correct since he was a child. As he recalled memories of a past life, simplified only by the painstaking process of living it, through it, beatings of such a father who didn't care to have a child who would exist in sociality, of a mother who wanted nothing but drugs and alcohol and who would die by the same beatings of the father.

Opening his eyes, The Mannequin stared across the café at the woman in the booth and saw her standing, walking to the door, leaving. She crossed the avenue, passing the next block into the alley and he smiled. Standing from the seat he was in, he reached into his jacket pocket and caressing the syringe filled with the dosage of chlorpromazine inside. Heading through the door outside he passed the street as the woman entered the alley, inhaling the fumes of the many cars that traveled the block and glancing over his shoulder, gave no indication away that he was to be stopped. His length of power was to continue and would forever reign upon the citizens of Duluth. People would fear him.

Reaching into the other pocket, this one filled with a second-choice weapon, he gripped the handle, and pulling out the blade, swiftly raised it in an arc as he charged the woman from behind.

A gunshot echoed through the alley, followed by a stabbing pain in his back. The Mannequin stumbled forward, his body twisting to the pavement and he turned his face towards the sky, the weapon in his hand slipping from his fingers as he felt it leave his hand. Whimpering in agony, he felt hot tears fill his eyes and blinked them away, scrambling to find what had happened. Turning his head towards the woman he saw her walking towards him, only the look on her face was of unquestionable malice. She knelt to pick up the blade and palming it, stepped towards him before crouching. Her hair fell in bangs over her eyes, shielding her gaze as the look in her features grew menacing.

A crunch of gravel and another person appeared in The Mannequin's view. He watched the dark haired, dark suited man crouch next to the woman, still holding the gun. He watched him smile.

"You know this game is only fit for two," he said, his voice cool, crisp and haunting. "Sorry to say you didn't make the cut." Turning to the woman he stepped back and she moved forward, inching closer. Before the Mannequin knew what had happened, she drove the blade home, into his left eye. The edge cut through brain tissue and nerves, and as he began to howl in agony, the man fired a round in his head, giving him a third eye.

Silence.

The two criminals walked away from the alley, leaving the body to be found hours later by police. News of The Mannequin's death spread over the news while in the hospital, Lieutenant Wayne Lovejoy's health continued to improve. Two officers were posted at his door round the clock so as not to repeat the incident with the technician. Deputy Chief Iris Hogan surveyed the concept that if Lovejoy didn't make it, she would need to appoint a new man in charge, but it was she who was watching the cases come and go through the system. Nothing was escaping her eye, as far as the murder of The Mannequin was concerned.

If one problem was solved, another would begin.

XXI |

Lincoln Sebastian sat down with his laptop and hesitated a moment before inserting the USB drive into the slot. He waited for the icon to reveal it was loading the drive and then clicking on the option panel, chose to open the folder to view the files. The drive wasn't very full, only a single MP4 was seen. It was labeled "mov.1" and the time allotted in the sidebar showed it ran for twenty-six minutes and thirty-nine seconds.

Taking a deep breath, Sebastian clicked on it.

The screen blinked, then grew dark. The icon for "Movies & TV" popped up before the laptop whirred. He watched the video start to play, revealing a black and white screening of what appeared to be a family in a yard. There was a mother and a father, with two young boys. The mother was seated on a lawn chair and the father was busy at the grille, cooking what appeared to be burgers and brats. The audio was clear, and he listened as he heard the man speak, the voice chilling as he remembered it from when he was a child.

"Boys now don't be too wild," the father said. "I don't need you to be up like last night." A smile played on his face, as if nothing was wrong, even though it seemed that it was. Turning to gaze into the camera as it focused on him, he shook his head and closed the grille, folding his arms while holding the tongs and staring back into the lens greeted the camera with a gleam in his eye. "So, you want to question me or just make me look bad?" he waited for the camera person to answer and then suddenly there was a loud bang followed by a scream and the lens turned suddenly, black and white spinning as the focus was turned upon the kids. One of the boys, the littlest, was on all fours, vomiting while the other, standing and holding his gut, was sobbing.

"Isaac!" Sebastian heard the mother scream. She ran into the picture. From the point of view that the camera caught the boy holding his gut was growing weak and as he sunk to his knees, his hands slipped from his chest and what was on the ground between the two boys was revealed, glistening in the sun.

A gun.

The picture changed, losing focus before switching. The camera was pointed at the father who was now seated in an armchair. He had his head held in his hands and was staring at the floor. His face was overcast, and Sebastian knew something had gone wrong. Something had happened that had caused this man to break. Only it wouldn't be for a time that he would realize his mistake of remaining where he was, shaded by a façade that would soon be shattered like little pieces of crockery.

Now, as he watched the lens remain in focus on the face, he heard noise in the background followed by quick footsteps before a woman came into view and using her hands as fists, beat the father in the back repeatedly.

"You left it out!" she screamed. "You left it out there in the open and he found it! He found the gun and he shot Isaac . . ." Her voice cracked and as the man allowed the blows to come, he fought them only at the end, taking her in his arms and then finally as she subdued to his welcome embrace, did tears start to flow from his eyes.

The camera changed again, becoming color. A video taken during a funeral. The pastor stood beside the casket as it was being lowered. Among the crowd were friends, family, people who had come to share their grief and respect. The man holding the camera trained his focus on the woman seated in the chair closest to the hole swallowing the coffin; her face was covered by a veil, yet he could see the blonde hair and the pale skin along with the red lipstick surrounding her mouth as it curled in disgust of what had happened. Beside her, a boy, one that Sebastian didn't recognize, sat with his hand in his mother's head forward, gazing unbeknownst to what was abound in surrounding him, and the camera trained itself on their laced fingers before fading to black.

An image materialized out of the film and Sebastian watched the news report reveal itself as if looking back on his own life entailed for it to be forgotten again.

". . . in other news today, Duluth, Minnesota police officer Shane Moriarty was pronounced dead at the scene of a horrific crime in which a young boy's mother was discovered murdered by none other than the son himself. Officer Moriarty was said to have been involved in the murder, while the boy's mother was innocent. Moriarty's family refused to press charges after the boy himself shot him with his father's gun. His father, Officer Bryce Sebastian has been put on suspension until further notice. The investigation has been postponed—"

The feed cut, and then refocused on a set of words that were typed into the screen. Beneath the words, the image of Officer Shane Moriarty remained rooted in the background.

YOU TOOK EVERYTHING I EVER CARED FOR FROM ME. NOW I WILL TAKE EVERYTHING FROM YOU. WHEN I AM FINISHED, THERE WILL BE NOTHING LEFT FOR YOU TO HAVE TO HOLD, TO KEEP, TO LOVE, OR TO CHERISH. I AM YOUR NIGHTMARE DETECTIVE SEBASTIAN. I WILL BE YOUR END.

The video ended and the words froze on the screen. Sebastian stared at the text for what seemed like a moment frozen in time; his mouth tasted sour and he could only imagine who he was up against and why they wanted anything to do with him, let alone know who he was. What he had done.

A creak in the floorboard and he reached for his gun, pointing it in the direction of the noise. Standing in the hall, clutching her robe around herself, Skye saw the look in his eyes, the look of a man who had finally lost control. She stared at him a moment, shocked at his move toward homicide and then blinking away the reprieve, stepped over the threshold of personal space and taking the gun from him, set it on the table after turning the safety on. Seating herself on his lap she turned his face to look at her and kissed him full on the mouth, sensually grinding her hips into his pelvis. She felt him rise, if only a little, but not enough to pleasure them both.

Meeting his eyes, she watched them remain fixated, on the screen.

"What is it that keeps you from having alone time with me?" she said.

"Protecting you," Sebastian said, and he closed the laptop, but not before closing the window and removing the flash drive, slipped it into his coat which was hung on the back of the chair. Reaching up to brush hair from her face he smiled, and she leaned her head into his hand. Pressing his forehead against hers, he breathed in her scent: a sweet lavender mixed with vanilla.

"If you want to protect me you should fuck me," Skye said. "I feel like we haven't laid in a day."

Sebastian chuckled. "It's been a day."

"You would know."

He raised his brow. "Oh, I would know? I thought you were in control?"

Skye giggled. Leaning over him she pressed her pelvis into his, feeling a higher rise. "You want me to be dominatrix?" she watched Sebastian smile, seeing a mischievous gleam in his eye. Suddenly, she was being lifted, up and then carried, over his shoulder, to the bedroom.

"Honey," he said, "*I'm the fucking Dom.*"

The door shut with a bang and a stillness filled the house. A ruckus followed of sudden emotion before a squeal of laughter from Skye.

"God," she moaned, "that's a mouthful."

XXII |

Early next morning, Sebastian received a call that Lieutenant Wayne Lovejoy's condition had improved: he was going to make it. As he sat up in bed, rubbing sleep from his eyes and turned to look at the occupant beside him, her form quiet as well as beautiful, Sebastian could only imagine how much farther this was going before he felt it would break him. The fact that the message on the flash drive had been pressing enough made him believe that the person who was after him held a grudge from his past and wanted to get in his way, to make him suffer. It was haunting to know that after three decades the vendetta was still a reality. It wouldn't end until one of them was dead.

Sebastian watched Skye stir in her sleep and then mumble something, still dreaming. He sighed, resting a hand on the small of her back, feeling the softness of her skin. She smiled, and her arm snaked out to feel for him, finding him. The other followed and she nuzzled her neck into the crook of his elbow, returning to rest.

Staring at the clock on the bedside table Sebastian saw it was only seven twenty-six in the morning. The lieutenant would still be sleeping. As he looked across the room, he watched the shadows move within the morning light filtering in through the blinds and heard the alarm clock switch on minutes later to the station that Skye had left it on. Taking Back Sunday sang "MakeDamnSure" and the tune filled the room, making him wonder how the lyrics had anything to do with the feelings of himself aside from the "break you down so badly" chorus.

Sebastian shook his head.

The past always caught up with you in the end. It would be fighting with you, destroying your façade and breaking you to pieces if you let it. As the song finished, he heard the noise of his bedmate groaning and the bed moving beside him woke his conscience. He quickly switched off the radio, hearing silence as he turned to look at her and she gazed at him, smiling tiredly.

"Hi," she said.

"Hi," he said.

Seeing the look on his face, Skye yawned. "Work?"

Sebastian nodded. "Yeah. The lieutenant's condition is bettering, and they say he's going to make it. They want me to go to the hospital and see him before meeting up with my partner to go over the file that the M.E. gave me on the case."

Skye propped herself up on her elbows, her gaze forlorn. "Do you have to go?"

Sebastian sighed. "Yeah. I'll be back sometime tonight. I promise." Standing from the bed he went to the bathroom and running the water in the shower waited for the warmth to flow. He heard footfalls behind him and turned to see Skye behind him, her hands pressing into his chest before they both stepped in the shower.

One last time of passion before a day on the job.

XXIII |

The hospital room was dimly lit, the curtains to the windows closed to keep light from violating the space. In the bed, Lieutenant Wayne Lovejoy breathed normally, albeit in pain, having been shot three times, all three targets missing vital organs. His bandages were redressed daily, the wounds checked and cleaned before being gauzed and covered once more. As the older man was visited by his two younger detectives, his eyes remained closed, if only for the moment, as he slept, having woken early in the morning to the guard who had checked on him to see how he was. Lovejoy had stirred so suddenly and opened his eyes in shock to see the man in black hovering over him, his heart rate monitor beeping loudly. The nurses had rushed in to see to it that he didn't go into cardiac arrest with his already weak heart. It took them a half hour, but they calmed him, and the call was given to Sebastian, per Lovejoy's orders. The man said his name repeatedly, wishing that the order be done.

"Call Detective Sebastian . . . call him."

As Sebastian stood beside the bed, watching the lieutenant rest, having been giving medication for pain as well as the panic, he glanced at his partner, seeing her gaze focused on the IV and the heart rate monitor, watching his pulse. Mallory glanced at him and shook her head, throwing her hands up as she said, "I can't be here right now." Turning she walked out of the room and into the hall and Sebastian watched her leave, heading to the nurse's station where she asked for the chart and looked it over, reading each page for names as to who had visited. Hearing a noise from the bed, something like a cough, he turned back to see Lovejoy's eyes open and the man gazing at the ceiling. His gaze turned to see him, and Sebastian smiled.

"How are you, sir?"

Lovejoy coughed again, hacking. Sebastian thought he might start to vomit by the way it sounded but after drinking from a bottle of water that was beside his bed, he was fine. His boss sighed. "Like hell," he said. A moment passed in silence as he stared across the room blankly. When he spoke, his tone was somber. "I was wrong, Lincoln."

"Sir?"

The lieutenant turned to his detective, meeting him with a meaningful stare. "I should have never let you off that case. It was wrong.

The reason the person is still after you is because you're off the investigation." He cleared his throat. "I'm putting you back on."

Sebastian felt a dreaded understanding but at the same time, relief. "What about Skye, sir?"

"They know she's a loose end," Lovejoy said, "like I said. They want her out of the game." He stared at him a moment. "Where is she?"

"At my house."

"As far as we know they don't have any clue as to where you live." The lieutenant nodded. "She'll be safe." He glanced beyond the door to the other detective. "How's she fairing?"

Sebastian looked to Mallory and saw her still reading the chart. "She's fine," he said. "I received a file a from the M.E. along with a flash drive. The flash drive contained a home video compilation video of Shane Moriarty and his family."

Lovejoy furrowed his brow. "Shane?" he shook his head. "You mean the dirty cop that you—?"

Sebastian bit his tongue, nodding. After a glance at Mallory he nodded, turning back to his boss.

"Yes," he said, "the dirty cop I shot when I was eight."

"Do you have any new information on him yet?"

"Just that he had two sons. One of them was killed when the other messed with a gun that he left out."

Lovejoy winced. "What was his name?"

"Isaac."

"The other's?"

"I don't know. It wasn't mentioned."

"Maybe the folder has something. Or the folder on Shane." Lovejoy reached for the remote to sit up and found air. Sebastian grabbed the device and handed it to him. "Thanks. So, I want you and Detective Grey on the case again. Working *together*. See what you can find on Shane. Is his wife still alive?"

"She died about four years ago from breast cancer."

Lovejoy pressed the switch to raise the bed and scooting up, grimaced as the pain shot up his chest before he grew comfortable and setting the remote down looked past Sebastian to the officers. "They here all the time?"

"They switch every shift."

"Hourly?"

"Don't want to make the same mistake as the tech," Sebastian said. He checked his watch. "I have the file on Moriarty from Dennison in my car. I'm going to the department's file room with Mallory to see what I can find on Shane's kid. You give a call if you need me here. Let me know in warning if something goes wrong. Skye has my number." He turned to go.

"Detective Sebastian."

Sebastian stopped, turning back to his boss.

Lovejoy stared at the man in his doorway.

"Good luck," he said.

Sebastian nodded. He said nothing. Leaving the room, he walked with Mallory back to his car before leaving the hospital and heading to the department, unaware that parked in the adjoining lot outside, an idling Range Rover was waiting, its driver watching the Audi as it peeled away from the curb with both detectives in tow.

Behind the wheel, the man stared coldly at the taillights, seeing them turn red before the car turned left up the next street and disappeared. Feeling his cell phone buzz in his pocket he pulled it out, staring at the message: a given address. Smiling he left the parking lot, heading up the hill, towards Piedmont.

XXIV |

After signing into the department's file room sheet, Sebastian and Mallory went through the rows of alphabetical cabinets to find the folder they were looking for and digging out two, assorted each other with going through one each and then the one the M.E. had given him together. As Mallory paced and read while Sebastian sat at his desk, going over the contents of the smaller compilation of history, they were surprised to find nothing that involved children aside from there being two that had been born to Shane and Charlotte Moriarty, one of which was dead, the other which had been labeled MIA and not seen ten years after his father's death.

"Here's something," Mallory said, walking to the desk. She set the folder she was holding down and pointed to a picture of Shane Moriarty and his wife along with two boys. "There's Shane and Charlotte. Isaac is the one on the left." She pointed to the blonde boy who was smirking into the lens, beaming a brightness that would gleam for only a few more years. "Do we know who the other brother is yet?"

"He went MIA ten years after Shane died," Sebastian said, shaking his head. "We still have the third file to go over yet." Grabbing the file, the M.E. had given him, he slid it to the center of the desk and pulling it open stared at the first page. It was a coroner's report to identify the body of the department's attacker. He stared at the name and realized that what he was looking at was the answer.

Seeing the look on Sebastian's face, Mallory asked, "What is it?"

"I think I know who the other brother was," Sebastian said.

"Who?"

"He's sitting in the morgue."

Mallory shook her head. "That's impossible. How could he have—" she saw the look on Sebastian's face and realized it was clear.

"He was sent by someone else," Sebastian said and stood, quickly grabbing his keys.

"Who?" Mallory said.

"The one who wanted me out of my house in the first place."

Starting after him, Mallory realized what he meant.

"Oh, my God," she said. "Skye."

XXV |

Skye Danes lay on the couch, strumming on her guitar, singing to the tune of Red Hot Chili Peppers' "Don't Forget Me" as she tapped her foot and thought about early days in life when her band had still been together and she had felt connected, knowing it was only a matter of time before she reached the point of breaking and it felt like the whole world was wanting what she could never give. It was as if she was fighting the reality that the nightmare of being where she was, stuck in some cover band, wasn't where she wanted to be.

Shaking her head, she thrummed the strings and felt her fingers play the beat as she listened to the tone of her voice and continued, knowing how she sounded was important to other people if she ever decided to join the band again. If they ever let her back in and it was something, she wanted more than anything, to be on the road once more, to feel the tug of emotion, to have the audience of a lifetime cheering for her.

Finishing, she started "The Zephyr Song" by the same band. Her feelings towards the beat of the music were moot and she didn't care to say how she was about singing it. Instead she just did and that was how it stayed.

A sudden draft of cool air filled the room and Skye heard the creak of a floorboard. Stopping her fingers on the strings she listened, hearing nothing but silence and glancing out the living room window, watched a minivan pass by on the street. In the driveway, the Audi was still gone. Sebastian wasn't home. Walking to the kitchen she dug in one of the drawers and finding a butcher knife, cradled the handle in her palm, keeping it at her side before glancing down the hall and turning to look at the back door saw the source of the air flow. Quietly she shut the entry, locking it with the deadbolt.

Click.

Skye heard the noise but didn't freeze. Spinning on her heels she raised the knife, poised to stab, a gloved hand grabbing the wrist and twisting it sharply, painfully. The blade fell from nerveless fingers and dropped to the floor. Staring into the stranger's face, she watched him smile, chuckling.

"You should know by now," he said, "never to bring a knife to a gun fight."

"Fuck you," Skye said.

The man's smile faded, and he released her, pointing the gun in her face. Skye backed up, pressing herself against the door. Her hand reached the knob and he shook his head.

"Don't even think about it."

Letting her hand drop to her side, the singer stared down the barrel, watching the finger ease on the trigger. As the dark eyes glared, she wondered if, inside them, there was still any sort of life left. After three decades, she wondered, if at all that there had been any at all to exist.

"What's the combination to the case?" he asked.

Skye curled her lip in disgust. "I don't know," she said.

The gun aimed to the left. A round was fired, and she felt a heated flame tear across the skin of her shoulder. Screaming in sudden pain, she gripped the wound and staggered, grabbing the counter with her free hand.

"Wrong answer." The man inclined his head. "What is the combination?"

Skye whimpered, staring out the window. Where was Sebastian? Looking back to the man she shook her head. "I'm serious," she said. "I don't know any combination. I don't know what you're talking about."

The man breathed through his nostrils loudly, angered. Biting his teeth together and grinding he narrowed his eyes into slits, and then pointing the gun at the singer's chest, pulled the trigger. Skye sunk to the floor, gripping her stomach. She looked up, her body in agony as she watched the stranger storm through the front door and straining to keep her eyes open, watched as slowly, everything became black.

Sebastian drove at a decent speed across roads that were paved, feeling as if his life depended on sanity, while at the same time, hearing the pounding abbreviation of panic passing through his blood and making itself known to him in a way that caused the heart in his chest to hammer against his ribs like a jackhammer.

"Do you think he might still be there?" Mallory asked.

Sebastian gripped the steering wheel with white knuckled fingers, staring straight ahead. He watched as, in passing, a black Range Rover honked its horn in response to him coming close to the other lane. He shook his head and didn't respond. As he reached the driveway, he turned sharply and felt the rear of his car fishtail on gravel before the front bumper pulled over the tar and he slammed on the brakes, pushing open the driver's door and not caring to shut it, ran up the path to the door, finding it yawning open. Drawing out his gun, he checked to make sure the safety was off, and glancing behind him, watched Mallory look over her shoulder before turning back to him, shaking her head. He took a deep breath, stepping over the threshold into his home and then, passing through the living room, listened to the sound of silence.

"Skye?"

There was no answer from the hall, and he turned to look down it before glancing into the kitchen. He saw the form of a body leaned against the back door and instantly knew who it was. Hurrying to Skye's aide, he checked for a pulse and found a weak beat of heart. Using his cell, he dialed for ambulance and was quick to see if she was still breathing. As he stared at the wound in her shoulder and the bigger damage done to her chest, he wondered if she would make it at all.

"Skye," he said, and touched her cheek, feeling the skin of her face soaked in not sweat, but tears. Tears he knew that had been shed in fear and sadness. Something he knew would lead to another matter entirely.

Trust.

"Skye."

Slowly, the singer's eyes fluttered open and she turned her head to look at him, her forehead creasing to a knitted brow and fresh tears poured from her eyes. Her lips moved; her mouth filled with mucus.

"You left me."

Sebastian winced inwardly at the remark. He heard footfalls behind him and turned to see his partner standing above him. Mallory gasped at the sight of the young woman and stepped back; her mouth covered. Looking back to Skye he saw her weakly reaching up to touch his hand. Feebly, she pushed it away.

"Skye," he said. "Skye, I'm sorry."

Distantly, Sebastian heard the sirens and he knew it was no use. As he stayed by her side and waited for the EMTs to arrive, he knew there was nothing he could do but accept the fact that he had failed her.

Skye would never forgive him.

XXVI |

One Week Later

Seated in the waiting room, Detective Lincoln Sebastian clasped his hands together and stared at the floor, awaiting the news for both his lover and his boss. The lieutenant had been cleared for release and Skye would be in for another month, going through physical therapy at another clinic. They hadn't talked since the incident at his house and since then he hadn't been able to forgive himself for allowing her safety to be at risk. It was something he knew he couldn't control, let alone the factor of it being a reality he risked and now it was out of his hands.

She would be leaving him to be alone like he was when she first met him.

Shaking his head, he breathed in deeply and exhaled heavily, glancing up only to see a desk clerk bringing over a chart to the station and then reading from it say a name that wasn't his, bringing someone else into the check-up area again before they saw the doctor.

A moment passed in stillness again and then he heard footsteps before seeing movement in his peripheral. The person sat down next to him and he felt a hand on his back, a soothing touch that didn't feel like it belonged to him; he felt he should be beaten.

"How are you doing?" his partner asked.

Sebastian glanced at Mallory, seeing her knitted brow. Only an hour ago she had been at the office, going over paperwork, seeing what they could find on the mysterious killer. The bullet pulled from Skye had been untraceable; a common placed round that was bought in any store—they had hit a dead end. The case was cold. In a few weeks, if Lieutenant Lovejoy chose, the investigation would be dropped.

"Detective Sebastian?"

Sebastian looked up. He saw the nurse beckoning. Standing up he strode through the doors, following the nurse through to the bedroom where Lovejoy was dressed and ready to go. He was tightening his tie and smoothing the lapels of his suit. Looking at Sebastian he stared.

"You look like hell, Lincoln."

"Thank you, sir."

"So, how is she?"

Sebastian shook his head. He scratched his scalp and stared at the floor. "She doesn't trust me as much as she did when we first met," he said. "She says I left her to die."

"You kind of did."

"I didn't know what he was capable of."

"No one did." Lovejoy finished signing the clipboard of pages from the nurse and sighed. "So glad to be out of this place. Thought I might die here."

"You're not dead yet, sir."

"Nope."

Sebastian glanced down the hall, hearing the distant beeping and shuffling papers and phones ringing. Looking at the nurse he nodded. The woman checked her clipboard and shook her head in.

"This way."

They walked the corridor to the elevator before taking it to another floor and getting off, walked to a room with a single bed where Skye was being watched by two officers who stood guarding the door in hourly shifts. She was hooked up to oxygen and her body was blanketed and had an IV line in her right arm, because her left was bandaged from the wound. When

Sebastian walked in to see her, she stared at him but said nothing.

"I know you don't care to see me," he said, "but I thought you should know that we have nothing as of right now on the case to work with. We don't know who the guy is and without a composite sketch of his face we have nothing for the system."

Skye continued to look at him but said nothing. He watched her swallow dryly. She reached out for her water and fumbling felt for the table. Sebastian grabbed it and handed it to her and she took it from him weakly, sipping from the open cap before screwing it back on and setting it on the table, glanced at the far screen of the television, watching the blank and empty void of the blackness. Sebastian turned and saw her reflected back, in the hospital bed and looking back knew it was pointless. He would get nothing out of the conversation. He turned to leave.

"You can still come and visit," Skye said. "If you really want to."

Sebastian stopped, remaining faced away. He listened to her breathing, shallow and soft.

"Still," she continued, "I don't want anything to do with you after I leave here."

He bit his tongue, fighting the urge to say something, anything. He felt the reason that she was mad at him growing like a tumor on his heart, waiting for the moment to cause failure, allowing the blackness to grow and the sickness within to kill him in finality.

Striding back down the hall he left through the stairwell, exiting the building and heading back to his car, slowed as he reached the parking lot. The Audi was parked where he'd left it, sitting facing the street. Tucked in between the windshield and the wipers, a piece of paper fluttered in the wind. Opening his trunk, Sebastian found a pair of gloves and donning them, took the new piece of evidence, staring at the red letters printed in bold across the page.

YOU WILL FAIL TO PROTECT HER IN THE END.

I WILL WIN.

Feeling a sudden chill, Sebastian stared up at the hospital building and watched the windows glint in the evening sunlight. As he turned back to the page, he knew it wasn't only a truth but reality.

The killer was not done with Skye.

The game had only begun.

| Part Three |

| September |

XXVII |

The warm weather stayed while storms moved in over Lake Superior. Fishermen stayed off the waters for some time after the whitecaps and the waves began to crash against shore. The canal became a challenge for some long liners and people who watched the boats coming in and out of harbor were of the few to witness the bridge as it rose to boats and ships as well as others who were sprayed by frothy swells that rose higher than normal over the canal's borders.

Standing on the Lakewalk and staring out at the tide coming in, crashing over the rocks before passing through to smooth over the pebbles and the beach, Detective Lincoln Sebastian felt the breeze of the coming fall rippling through his trench coat which blew back behind him like a cape behind his legs. He didn't shiver, and he didn't bite his teeth together against the odd temperatures of the month in which was considered the worst forecast in Duluth, Minnesota history.

A car door was heard shutting from the parking lot followed by feet running along the plank boarding. Sebastian didn't turn his head but knew who it was as he stepped closer to the beach and allowed the next wave to fill the void, spraying him with drops of lake water.

"I thought I'd find you here," Detective Mallory Grey said.

"Did Lovejoy tell you?"

"No. I knew already where you'd go." Taking a deep breath to gain her composure, Mallory stared at the waves coming in and said, "You really want to be here right now? The lake's coming in and despite what the weather says, this stuff is gonna get worse over the next week or so. We're supposed to have thunderstorms."

Sebastian nodded. "Some." He looked at his watch.

"What are you waiting for?"

"Time to stop."

"For who?"

Sebastian cleared his throat. "Me. I'm tired of this job. I hate working for something that doesn't lead anywhere. There's been nothing since that note on my car and I haven't seen a sign that he's making a move."

"You're hoping he shows his face."

He turned to look at her, seeing the way she squinted against the breeze. Her eyes seemed to twinkle and behind them, something else, something out of place. He frowned, then turned, walking back towards the lot. Standing next to his Audi he wondered how Skye was doing. Lately she had been working on writing new music. After the incident she had gotten a call from her bandmates who had told her she was welcome back in if she wanted. Yris had given her another chance at fame and Skye took the bait. She was in between therapy and singing, the doctor sure to warn her about the strain it would put on her heart. Sebastian had been there when she had received the news and she had looked at him, ignoring the advice as she told him her response.

"It's already broken."

Now, standing under the unforgiving plight of the investigation he was in, Sebastian felt it was pointless. Staring at the water he watched Mallory stare at him before getting back into his car and driving to the department where he went to his office, sitting at his desk to pore over the file from the M.E. for the hundredth time. Even if he found nothing, he knew it wasn't for naught. He felt that there was still something to do now that he had everything at stake.

Skye's life was still in danger.

XXVIII |

Skye Danes sat in a chair on stage, tuning her guitar. At the end of the last song she had felt the tug of fatigue and told her bandmate Toby she wanted to pass the torch of bass player to Sasha and have keyboard separate from the next beat on another tune they were going to be singing. All the while, in her mind, she was thinking about Sebastian. The detective had kept a hold on her for some time and she couldn't forget about his face, how he cared for her despite that she wanted nothing to do with him.

Focusing on the concert, which was at Clyde Iron Works in West Duluth, she had gotten through most of the show, but her shoulder had felt like it was on fire and her chest still hurt. Against doctor's orders she had left the hospital earlier than was wise and gone on with Yris to do a new show which was sold out, the crowd ecstatic to see her and after everything that had happened with the break up and the band getting back together, Skye was willing to give it her all.

Hearing a catcall from across the stage, Skye looked up and turned to face the oncoming fan who was walking up to meet her with excited tension. The young woman smiled, giving her a sudden hug and as Skye winced frowned in panic.

"Sorry," she said. "Injuries, right?" the girl appeared nervous and tucked a strand of pink hair from her eyes behind and ear. Her gray colored eyes viewed her with kindness, and she watched Skye smile in return.

"I'm all right," she said. "You enjoy the show?"

Jumping up and down the woman squealed. "I loved it!" she covered her mouth to stifle the noise of another piercing ejaculation of glee and pointed at the singer. "I love what you did with your hair. It looks nice."

Skye took a strand of her bleached white hair and smoothed her fingers through it. "Thanks," she said. Adding as an afterthought, she asked, "Do you want a picture?"

The fan, obviously intrigued, beamed. She nodded frantically and grabbed her phone, passing it to Skye who took it and passed it to Toby. Taking her guitar, she removed the strap from her shoulder and passed the torch to the woman. "Here, you can hold it in the photo."

"Really?"

"Sure."

Pulling the guitar strap over her head the fan positioned herself in Skye's embrace as the singer put her arm around her shoulder and Toby used the phone to take three pictures, the two women in various poses, always signing "rock on" with their hands. Skye looked at the phone and the photos taken and smiled.

"You're lucky my bassist is such a good shot," she said. As she watched the woman start to remove the guitar from her shoulder, she nodded to her and added, "Keep it."

The fan, shocked, asked, "For real?"

"Yeah. Consider it a backstage present. I'll even sign it."

As she took a marker and wrote her name beneath the strings, Skye felt the feeling that this was going to be a moment she would never forget, a time when, for once, she wasn't thinking about Sebastian. She knew she could let him go eventually, but if it dragged on her that he was a part of her life, that she still loved him, she felt she would never be able to forgive herself for letting him slip through her grasp.

The one man who got away.

"Thank you so much," the woman said. She hugged Skye again, this time more gently. Skye smiled as she was released and realizing she hadn't gotten her name, asked.

"It's Ginger," the woman said. "Ginger Cornell."

"Have a rockin' day, Ginger," Skye said. She watched her leave and then turned back to see Toby standing on the stage, his arms folded, smiling. "What?"

"That," he said, "has got to be the best thing you've done for a fan since the founding of Yris."

"It wasn't stupid."

"I never said that."

A pause. "What do you see in that detective?"

Skye caught her lip between her teeth, biting it. At first didn't reply. Then, as the words came to her, she spoke them and was surprised to hear herself say them.

"Someone who feels as helpless as I do."

XXIX |

Sebastian felt tired but continued to push himself as he read through the gathered report on the murders involving the Verso Company. The deaths of Sean Miller, Seth Kent, and Ryan Rayburn had all been revolved around a missing file folder that had burned up in the blast that killed Sean Miller. When the technician that had been poisoned through his IV had been stopped on the highway and shot, the remains of the document had been stolen and never found. What was in the folder that Miller had been protecting Sebastian couldn't find and he knew his best bet at discovering facts on the matter would be to dig into the company's system.

That might take days. Or weeks. Or months. Or years.

Looking at his watch, Sebastian realized it was useless to go any further in depth and as he yawned, stretching as he stood, he closed the file and sliding it into his desk, left his office, locking up for the day. He headed to see if Lovejoy was in and found his door locked. Turning to his secretary's desk he asked Katie, "Is he in?"

"He left for the day," she said. "He'll be back tomorrow."

Heading out to his car, Sebastian drove to the mall and Barnes & Noble, taking a seat in the café after ordering a hot chocolate. Outside the large windows the day had darkened, and the clouds in the sky had grown black, heavy with their burden of rain. As he listened to the storm of thunder in the distance, he closed his eyes, taking a breath and then hearing footfalls coming towards him opened them to see his partner, Mallory, walking over, carrying a hardcover in her hand. She smiled as she met his eyes and he stared back, drowsy yet still awake.

"Hi," she said, "fancy meeting you here."

"Yeah," he said. "I would say the same thing." He yawned a second time. "If I wasn't so groggy."

"You sleep well enough?"

"Yeah. I just can't seem to get my head around this case. It's like the trail's run cold and there's nothing more to be found. I can't find anything on who this guy is or why he wants anything to do with me and who he is from my past. Or who this woman is that's working with him."

Mallory took a seat across from him and set the book down, smoothing her hand over the cover and gazing at him knowingly wondered what he thought about her own imagination. She blinked as they both heard thunder roll and then suddenly rain slashed against the windows in a torrent, filling the store with a loud roar of water against glass. A sudden boom of a second charge of thunder and then out of nowhere, the store lights flickered, the entirety of Barnes & Noble going dark.

"Just great," Sebastian said, staring into the black. He saw a flash of light and heard people scream as well as kids cry before the beam of light showed on his face. He recognized Mallory's in the glow of her phone as she smiled.

"Awkward, huh?" she said.

"Yeah."

"Never happened before as far as I'm concerned."

"Never before since I've been here."

"You think they'll come back on?"

As if on cue, the lights flickered, switching on one by one. The store glowed and Mallory glimpsed the look of relaxation on Sebastian's face. He stared at the cup in his hand and took a slow sip before shaking his head.

"Damn Minnesota power," he said.

XXX |

A day passed and then two. Skye took a week's reprieve at a motel downtown and Sebastian was made aware, coming to check on her the very same afternoon. It was a quieter evening, warmer than usual. The stormy weather had moved farther South towards the cities and Duluth was a comfortable shade of yellow in the sunshine. It wasn't to last is what the weatherman said. The rain would return by October before the snow and there would be no stopping the cold front from blowing in.

As he entered the Holiday Inn Hotel, he found the pool area vacant save for a single swimmer doing laps. The person dove deep before coming back up and pushing off the wall, swam to the shallow end. Sebastian watched as Skye took the stairs, her two-piece black bikini revealing her athletic form and pierced navel, the glistening diamonds beading with water as she grabbed the towel from the chair beside the pool and wincing, favored her right arm as she wiped running water from her back and then tied the towel around her waist.

"Skye," he called.

She turned, fully, to face him and he saw the scar in her chest, right where the bullet had pierced her abdomen. She stared at him for a moment then walking to meet him stood a few feet away, said, "Yes?"

"I came to check on you."

She furrowed her brow in confusion and then seeing the seriousness on his face the look faded. "I'm fine." She turned, heading to one of the sliding doors of the hotel rooms. Pulling one open, she stepped inside, leaving it ajar. As he waited a moment he listened as he heard the distant sound of water running and then passing the threshold, came across into the suite and found her standing topless, her bare breasts showing hard pink areolas. He blinked, turning away.

"Oh, sorry."

Softly, and with a kindness he hadn't heard in a while, she said, "It's fine. It's nothing you haven't seen." She added, "Is there anything on the case that you've been able to find? Something new you can work on to investigate and find out who shot me?"

Sebastian swallowed dryly. It sounded firm, and serious, the way she said it. As he watched the wall, he saw her shadow and listened to movement before hearing her feet padding towards him, and she appeared, wearing a robe. She looked at him and he noticed her hair was bleached white.

"No," he said, finally. "There's nothing."

Skye sighed. "Let me know if you find something," she said. Stepping back to the shower he heard the door to the bathroom shut and then listened to the water run and knew the conversation was over. Walking back to his car he left the hotel, going to the department where he sat at his desk and pondered the fact that in only a few more days the case would be shut down.

There would be nothing he could do.

A knock sounded at his office door.

"Come in." Sebastian saw Lieutenant Lovejoy standing on the threshold, the man's gaze upon him, wearing a grim façade.

"Hi, sir. I know we haven't made progress, but . . ."

"You've made plenty," Lovejoy said. He shook his head. "The only problem is that we both didn't see what was right in front of us all along."

Sebastian furrowed his brow. "What's that, sir?"

Lovejoy folded his arms across his chest, albeit feeling the tightness there. He looked at his detective with newfound clarity of the mind. "You remember that Shane Moriarty only had two sons, right?"

"Yes, and both are dead."

"Both of the *blood related* are dead," Lovejoy said. He waved a finger in the air. "When Isaac Moriarty passed, it was a torn hole in the relationship between Shane and Charlotte and a bigger hole in their lives. So, they adopted."

Sebastian frowned, staring at his boss. It was too easy to be a mistake. Also, it was easily overlooked.

"Sir," he said, "you're saying that the man who is out there, the killer, he's the adopted child."

"Not only him," Lovejoy said. His face took on a look of worrisome contempt. "When the department searched its files for officers it never thought it would find a hole in the system. It appears that Mallory Grey isn't who she says she is."

Sebastian felt the air grow cold.

His own partner was the sibling to a killer who had been tracking him all along. She had been giving him away.

"Where's Skye?" Lovejoy asked.

Just as Sebastian was about to answer, his cell rang and he picked it up, staring at the caller ID. He recognized Skye's number and as he answered, he listened to the sound of breath on the other end of the line. He waited before clearing his throat and said, "This is Sebastian."

"Hello, Detective," the voice said, sounding crisp and slightly accented. "How does it feel to lose control of everything and still somehow have something you can grasp, something you feel you can hold? Imagination is so vital, isn't it?"

"Where is she?" Sebastian asked. "Where's Skye?"

A low chuckle and the voice clicked its tongue. "Tsk, tsk. You should know manners. After all you took something from me. Now I'm taking something from you."

"*Where—is she?!*"

"If you want her back, you'll have to meet my associate. I'm certain you know her already. You've worked with her for the past few months. Has it been that long?"

"*Where?*" Sebastian breathed.

"Two days. Great Lakes Aquarium. The large tank. Main floor viewing area. She'll be there. Have the combination. Or I'll put a bullet in her skull."

Click.

XXXI |

Day 1

Standing in his kitchen, drinking a bottle of Miller Lite beer, Sebastian stared at the floor, hearing the radio play on the counter, a tune of something he didn't recognize but which was somber and brooding. An unwelcome feeling brought together to make him believe he had allowed this to happen. It wasn't his imagination as Spencer Myron had made him believe. The man's name had come up in the file. He didn't carry the same last name as Shane Moriarty since he had kept his mother's maiden when moving in with the family. Mallory, his partner, had been a piece he was still unable to solve. Her connection with Myron was solid and with what the records had been collecting in phone calls, she had made several to an unknown cell traced back to Myron's number. It had been left in Sebastian's own after he called to give him the message and the warning.

Drinking another swig of beer, Sebastian felt his heart sag and wondered if he would ever truly be able to stop the mad man from his past. A ghost. If he could find it in himself to defeat the one thing that still haunted him these past three decades, or if it would destroy him in the end and Skye would die.

Staring at the far wall and the back door where he had found her after realizing the imminent danger inflicted after Myron discovered where he lived, Sebastian felt his throat tighten and his eyes burn and knew that if the tears came it would only make him feel the pressure and that if he let them flow, release the pain after all this time, he would never forgive himself for breaking.

The first salty bead streaked his face and he tasted it as it touched his lip. Dropping the bottle, he heard it hit the floor but not break, rolling away empty. Covering his face, he sobbed, sinking against the fridge. All the anger and the anguish came together to make him feel what he hadn't in so long. The once hardened shell of a man had broken, and he cried. He cried for his mother, murdered when he was only a child, he cried for his father, a man crippled by the law that he had fought for until the very end, but most of all, he cried for the fact that his existence, and Skye's would only remain if he finished what he'd started.

The case had to end.

Sniffling, Sebastian stared at the door and then looked at the empty bottle, feeling the weight of everything that had come down to this and he would do what he had started out to do.

He was going to protect Skye, and he would make sure Myron never hurt anyone ever again.

Standing up and taking the empty bottle, he tossed it in the recycle bin and headed to the bathroom, looking at himself in the mirror as he caught a glimpse of his red rimmed eyes. His age showed but he didn't deny his strength. Even after all this time his father had been right. It wouldn't matter how hard they broke you down, he had told him, you had to fight to get back on top. That was how it worked.

Returning to the kitchen, Sebastian watched the light of the day as it faded to night and knew that the first twenty-four hours had come and gone.

One more day, he thought.

The house was clean and furnished. Skye sat, unbound, in an armchair, staring across the living area at the man watching her with interest and a gleam of mock satisfaction in his eye. She listened to the sound of noises in the kitchen and watched cars passing by on the street outside the window. She didn't know where they were, but she felt a longing to be bold. Smiling she inclined her head, watching the man scowl.

"What's so funny?" he said.

"He's going to win," Skye said. "You're scared of him, that's the only reason you haven't done anything."

The man shifted in his chair, glaring at her from where he sat, then looking past her, watched the woman enter the living room, carrying two steaming mugs. She handed one to him. Skye recognized her hair and eye color, but knew it wasn't the person she thought she had trusted.

"Hello, *Detective*," she said. "Let me guess, he paid you to work for him."

Mallory Grey smiled and setting down her mug, pushed her fingers through her hair, pulling off what was the wig of burgundy hair. Blinking she removed the contacts and revealed ocean blue eyes, staring at Skye. The singer stared at her blonde hair.

"Actually," Mallory said, "I have been working with him from the beginning. We're a team. I trust him more than you know." She turned to the man and sitting in his lap locked lips, kissing hungrily before the man looked at her and watched Skye speak.

"You're both insane," she said.

"That's a compliment," he said. Looking to Mallory he said, "Take our guest to her room. Make sure she stays there for the next twenty-four hours. We won't be leaving until I make the call."

Mallory stood and reaching out, grabbed Skye by her left arm firmly, pulling her to her feet. The singer gasped in sudden pain and followed the dirty cop up the steps. Behind her she saw the man seated in the chair, waving.

"Have a good rest, Skye," he said. "Be sure to say your prayers."

She tripped on the first step before continuing up the next several and then down the hall, to the first bedroom on the left. Mallory opened the door and pushed her in, closing it behind her and locking it with a key. Skye looked around her and saw only the bed with sheets in one corner and a window beside it. Going to where the bed was, she laid on it and stared at the ceiling, thoughts of Sebastian breaking in as she felt a longing for him, wishing she could see him, wishing that when this was over, that she felt she could forgive him.

It wasn't his fault that she had been left behind. He didn't know that Mallory was against him; it was his partner's fault not his. Skye felt a distance between her and the dirty cop as if it was a destiny to do something drastic, and when the time came, she would know.

Closing her eyes to sleep she felt it take her away into dreams and she slumbered peacefully, memories of times when Yris had first been a band fading from picture as she remembered when she first saw Sebastian in the crowd and her father's death became known. The fact that the detective had loved her, and she didn't know was shocking, but at the same time it was a feeling she felt towards him as well.

She still cared about him; she just didn't believe it.

XXXII |

Day 2

Sebastian spent the last day formulating a plan. If things went wrong, he would be prepared. He knew that when he received the call and was told what time to meet, he would be ready. It was only a test of strength and will.

Standing in his kitchen he stared at the back door, feeling his body grow tense. Taking a deep breath, he heard the phone ring. Picking it up from its cradle, he answered.

"Sebastian."

"Hey, Lincoln, it's Lieutenant Lovejoy," his boss said. "You hear anything yet?"

Sebastian looked at his right hand, clenching his fingers tightly and then easing the white-knuckle tension to spread his palm he stared, and the blood flowed freely, growing its usual shade of deep pink. "No," he said.

"You're supposed to meet with him in a day, right?"

"Sir, I'm handling this on my own."

"Lincoln, you know it's one of those things that I can't clear. If they kill Skye—"

"They won't," Sebastian said. "I'll get him before he does."

"How can you be sure? You don't know what he's capable of. He's survived this long without crossing your path."

"He's bold, I'll give him that." Staring at the back door, Sebastian felt a tug on his conscience, telling him that it was nearing the limit to which he was willing to accept the matter as ludicrous. "Sir, please, just give me this."

Lovejoy sighed. "Okay," he said. "But if you don't get him—"

"Believe me," Sebastian said. "I will."

In the dark of the bedroom, Skye watched the shadows form and shift on the ceiling, thinking of the song "Unwell" by Matchbox Twenty which talked about making friends with the ones on the wall. She sighed, turning on her side, realizing it was useless not to try and rest. As she closed her eyes to rest, she blinked and then a moment later, heard a key turning in the lock and opening her eyes, saw daylight instantly. The door to the bedroom opened and Mallory stood there, holding her gun in hand. Pointing it at the singer she inclined her head.

"Get up," she said, "it's time to go."

XXXIII |

Sebastian stood outside his house and stared at the overcast of gray in the sky, the clouds mixing to become a mass of darkly shrouded paint in the ceiling of which he was below. He knew that rain would soon fall, and it would come down hard. As he listened to the silence, he waited a beat before walking to his car and getting behind the wheel started the engine. Backing out of the driveway, he steered towards Piedmont and the freeway, heading into the traffic that led to Canal Park and the aquarium.

XXXIV |

Skye stood with Mallory Grey under the viewing area on the main floor beneath the large tank that was one of the aquarium's attractions. As she stared at the woman's frustrated gaze, she watched her eyes narrow while she looked at her phone, seeing her dial the number again, and placing the phone to her ear, listen to it ring before going to voice mail.

"What is he ignoring you?" she said smartly and smiled.

Turning to Skye, Mallory glared and being sure not to pull her gun which was in the holster at her hip, so as not to draw attention, she shoved her cell back into her pocket, shaking her head.

"Just remember," Skye said. "You fucked up big time."

"Shut up."

"Just saying."

"I said *shut up.*"

Watching Mallory step sideways to view the path leading to the doors Skye saw her coat shift and noticed the gun in the holster, in plain view and within reach. Behind her the large tank housed the walled in view that was merely thick layered glass. She noticed the stain of water that had leaked and looked back at the gun in Mallory's holster. Mallory turned to stare at her and saw her gazing in the direction of the fish tank.

"What?"

Skye shrugged.

"Nice view."

Mallory squinted, confused and then stepped back a few more feet into the viewing area.

Skye followed suit, keeping close to her, waiting for the moment when the coat would shift, and the gun would be in view.

XXXV |

Sebastian pulled into the parking lot after flashing his badge to the man at the booth. He waved him on, and Sebastian pulled into a spot a few spaces away from a red Toyota Camry.

Mallory Grey's car.

Walking briskly to the doors, he stepped through and into the lobby, seeing the escalators in front of him, leading up to the second-floor viewing area. As he stared at the falling water and turned to look in the shop on his right, he saw no one he recognized.

Getting on the escalator, he rode it to the second floor.

XXXVI |

Standing under the tank, Mallory Grey was on alert. She kept her eyes on both sides of the open walkway that led past the viewing area. Checking her phone, she saw it was nearing noon. Already she wondered where Sebastian might be and as she watched the people passing by, saw Skye staring at her.

"He's coming," she said.

"No shit, Sherlock," Mallory said. "You wanna dig a little deeper?"

XXXVII |

Sebastian took the steps down and strode past the seal exhibit. Up ahead was the viewing area and in the center of the floor, the large tank towered the two stories of the building. He took a deep breath and easing his finger on the safety of his gun, drew the weapon out, holding it in front of him as he stepped forward to intercede.

XXXVIII |

Screams erupted through the aquarium as Mallory judged her next move. She reached for her gun, pulling aside her coat as she accounted for only her hand grabbing the weapon, but as Skye reached for it first, both women held the grip and with the safety off, Skye's finger touched the trigger, the singer aiming the gun away from the crowd of people.

"You bitch!" Mallory screamed as she forced her hand but was overpowered. Skye squeezed off four rounds, all of which emptied into the tank. As a hollow cracking sound issued forth from the damaged glass, Skye released the weapon and as the crowd that was running away from the chaos in panic towards the door swallowed her up, Mallory stared up to see the crack start to widen, before opening her mouth to scream again.

The second cry never made it past her lips.

The large tank ruptured, 85,000 gallons of water rushing out and flooding the entire floor.

As aquarium staff watched in horror of what their mistake had been to *not* fix the leak, even though a gun had caused the fracture in the glass, Mallory Grey pushed into the adjoining exhibit across from the viewing area, unconscious from the flow as it had come down upon her.

Sebastian ran for the safety of the stairs and made it as the tank continued to empty its contents, while families and children who were still in the building witnessed the horror of the large velocity within as it was drained of its glory.

As soon as the tank was empty, if with a little bit of water still left where the glass still resisted to contain the remaining fish, Sebastian stepped down, knee deep in the pool of standing water. A sturgeon floated past, darting by his leg and he quickly strode through, heading to where the exhibit area had swallowed up Mallory. He found her seated against a wall, her eyes closed and arms at her sides, gun nowhere to be found. Checking for a pulse, he found one, healthy and normal. Looking behind him, he found a man and calling him over instructed him to call an ambulance. Hurrying to the doors he stepped outside, looking over the parking lot. He found many cars that had been there were now gone, save for his Audi and a single Range Rover. The windows were tinted, and the car sat idling. As the taillights flashed, he watched the vehicle reverse before steering sharply, driving through exit. He recognized the make and model, remembering the passing SUV that he'd seen while driving to his house the day that Skye had been attacked.

Getting in his car, he followed the Range Rover, three car lengths behind. As the first car turned, he watched the SUV turn into Canal Park and then merge with traffic going across the Park Point bridge. Easing on the brake, he stared at the taillights of the vehicle and saw the hazards start to flash before the passenger's side door opened and Skye jumped out, heading for the bridge. Sirens could be heard, warning of a ship passing through the canal.

Sebastian watched the arm come down as the singer climbed the concrete sidewalk to the bridge, Spencer Myron getting out of his car and following close behind. The man ran after her, chasing her to the stairs where she was already over the gate and up the first flight. Getting out of his car and drawing his gun, Sebastian ran at a brisk pace, reaching the arm just as he saw the bridge start to rise. He jumped, landing on the opposite sidewalk as he looked down, watching the ground disappear beneath him and then grabbing onto the railing heard Skye yelling above him and turning to the adjoining flight of stairs opposite the ones the two had ascended, begin to climb.

XXXIX |

Skye breathed the chill air and felt her lungs burning, her chest thrumming with the beat of her heart as she took the final flight of stairs and passed the booth where the bridge operator was manning the controls. The man in the window didn't notice her as she waved to him, his attention to his work. A shot rang out, echoing through the beams and she looked down once, seeing the height at which she was, noticing the cruise ship entering the canal. Hearing the clink of shoes beneath her on the steps below she continued past the edge and seeing the end, noticed the gap between the crossing slats. She pushed her arms between them, edging her body to get through and as she placed her feet on the bridge's structure, felt her right heel slip, gripping tight with her left arm. She felt the strain and cried out, reaching out for the second beam with her other hand and finding it, heard another gunshot, this one closer. The heat of a bullet passed by her abdomen and she saw Myron, and continued to climb, fully aware of the distance between them, and at the same time wondered where Sebastian was.

Reaching the top of the structure, she pulled herself up and looked back, over the edge to the water, and saw the brown churning swells of the canal below. Looking out over Lake Superior, she saw whitecaps in the distance as the waves came into the shore. Catching her breath, she closed her eyes, feeling the cold bite at her arms and she shivered.

Click.

Skye heard the noise and felt reality dawn on her, a gust of wind tearing through her clothes, threatening to rip her away from the bridge and toss her into the current below. She turned slowly to face the man holding the gun and watched Myron's features tighten grimly into a scowl of rage.

"You caused all this trouble," he said. "For what? So, you could escape?" he pointed his gun at her chest. "I don't think so."

"Spencer!"

Skye watched her kidnapper turn as he heard the voice and looking up, saw Sebastian who stood on the opposite side of the bridge's structure. She watched the two stare each other down, a fight, that was no doubt, three decades in the making. Myron kept his gun trained at the other man's chest and smiled.

"So," he said, "you finally figured it out."

"You were never a part of the family," Sebastian said. "You were just in it." He looked at Skye, shaking his head. "When Shane died, you shadowed your brothers' intuition to get revenge for what I did."

"*You killed him!*" Myron yelled. "You shot him in cold blood and left him to die."

Sebastian shrugged, keeping his gun aimed true at the man before him. "He was a dirty cop. He deserved to be put down."

Myron snarled. "You son of a bitch!" he squeezed his finger on the trigger, firing off two rounds. Both bullets missed their targets.

Sebastian shot three times, hitting Myron in both shoulders and once in the chest. Skye watched the weapon in her kidnapper's hand drop, clattering between the slats of the bridge before striking the platform below. Myron stumbled backwards, losing his footing before falling from the top of the bridge. Sebastian watched as he grabbed at air, flailing, before splashing into the current that filled the canal.

·　　·　　·

The shock of cold water jolted Spencer Myron from his sudden daze. His shoulders felt on fire and his chest inflamed. He gagged on mouthfuls of the filthy water that surrounded him, fighting the surge of current rushing at him and as his body was dragged into the tow of the coming vessel, he suddenly became aware of the loud hum of the engine. Feeling himself caught in its flow, Myron kicked wildly, his gloved fingers groping the aqua that filled his vision. His trench coat trailed behind him, as it was caught in the blades, and he was pulled back into the churning maw of the vessel's engine.

People on both sides of the canal who watched the boat pass through screamed. From above, Sebastian and Skye heard the groan of the motor and watched the waters run red with blood from Myron's body caught in the propeller. Skye closed her eyes, turning to Sebastian and he put an arm around her, all the while watching the shreds of cloth float to the surface, lazily drifting in the canal.

Sebastian sighed.

After thirty-three years, it was over.

Spencer Myron, the ghost, the enemy that had tortured him for three decades, was gone.

| One Week Later |

| Monday |

XL |

The door to the interrogation room opened and Lieutenant Wayne Lovejoy stepped in, taking a seat across from Mallory Grey, AKA Bree Graves. The once burgundy haired detective was now blonde haired and ocean eyed, but thinner than usual. Since the incident at the aquarium she hadn't eaten much and the people at the facility holding her had told the department she had refused medication for the symptoms caused by sickness in relativity to contact with bacterial from the fish.

"So," Lovejoy said, "I'm here to speak with you about a deal."

Bree glanced up from her cuffs and fidgeting fingers to stare at her former boss. Her eyes appeared sunken, blackness under them. She spoke, her voice a rasp.

"I don't do deals," she said. "Just let me die."

The lieutenant stared at the woman and watched her eyes become glassy. "That's not an option," he said. "Either you can work with us or you go back to jail." He folded his hands in front of him on the table and cleared his throat. "What can you tell us about Spencer Myron?"

Bree glanced at the clock on the wall and saw the time. She looked back at Lovejoy.

"I want to go back," she said.

"Back where?"

"To jail."

Breathing a sigh, Lovejoy pushed back from the table and a moment later an officer came in, taking her by the arm and lifting her out of the chair. It was at this moment that Bree reacted. The former detective pushed back in the chair, dragging the cop back with her, and against the wall. Her hand reached for his holster and grabbing his gun, pointed it at the lieutenant. Lovejoy grabbed for his weapon, watching as Bree, instead of shooting him, put the barrel in her mouth and squeezed the trigger, the back of her head exploding, spraying brain matter and blood over the interrogation room.

"Damn," the officer said, standing as he reached for his gun.

"Don't touch that," Lovejoy said.

The man looked at his boss and asked, "Why?"

The lieutenant stared at the body of the woman who had once worked in the department, seated in the chair, her life over at the bite of a bullet.

"It's evidence," he said.

| Tuesday |

| Wednesday |

| Thursday |

| Friday |

XLI |

Sebastian sat at his desk, two weeks after taking leave. Since Skye had gone to the cities again to rehearse for a show that was taking place at Pizza Luce in Downtown Duluth, he had since retrieved the case from Spencer Myron's car and had been at work trying to open it. He thought of every possible combination and then realized as he sorted through each filed document that it was clear it could have been a simple as Skye's birthday which he tried, and it didn't work.

Looking at the document on Shane Moriarty he saw his birth year and day and wondered.

09-11-42.

Putting in the combination, Sebastian heard the discernible click as the latches popped. He opened the case to look inside finding a single sheet of paper, handwriting legible only to the naked eye of a man who was capable of such possible credentials and factual references. He stared at the signature and saw the familiar name of Kyle Danes. All at one he realized what it was.

Careful to keep the evidence clean and intact, he handled it with gloves and looked over the words, knowing that it was only certain he kept this quiet. He knew she would never understand that the truth behind her father's reason for allowing what happened to transpire and her to go with it was something that she would have to deal with. He had handled everything the best he could.

Sealing the letter back in the case he was sure to put it in evidence and then taking his car, drove to Pizza Luce where already, the show was on, and Yris was playing, singing a cover of "Times Like These" by Foo Fighters. As he passed through the crowd, coming up to the center, he watched Skye match the tone of Dave Grohl and the song flow through her in tone and lyric as well as melody.

The crowd cheered as she finished, and their eyes met. She stared at him and he watched her, knowing how she felt. He saw her speak into the mic.

"This next song," Skye said, "is for someone special in my life. He's saved me more times than I know." Pulling the guitar over her shoulder she tightened the strap and as her fingers found the strings, she said, "This song is called "With Me" by Sum 41."

The crowd whooped and people cheered. As Skye started to play the strings, Sebastian felt a sudden lift of his heart and watched as she started to sing. Her voice filled the room and she looked at him and came up an octave, continuing to play the guitar, and the chorus came, filling the room, her eyes never left him; she sang, belting out the song. He felt the love he had for her flow through him as she continued.

The emotions flowed and she thrilled him with the moment, the famous tune played by the band he could only remember hearing about but never thought had been as bright and poetic as this, to hear it sung by her voice—it was magic.

Skye thrummed her fingers on the guitar and as the rest of the band joined the chorus the crowd howled, whistling. Many saws who she was watching. A few clapped him on the back and one of them, a man, said, "She really cares about you to dedicate this song."

Sebastian only nodded. As the last chord was played, he walked up to the stage and Skye looked down before removing her guitar. She crouched to meet him, and he pulled her to him, lifting her in his arms and they kissed in the spotlight of the stage as the crowd looked on. There was no question about it.

After the investigation's conclusion and his dedication to protect her, there wasn't a doubt in Skye's mind that she felt the connection was real. For Sebastian it was the same. The case had torn them apart, but they had learned something about being together, and the fact that it had brought them closer, meant everything to them.

They had found each other.

That was all that mattered.